I FUNNY

JAMES PATTERSON is the internationally bestselling author of the highly praised Middle School books, *Homeroom Diaries*, and the I Funny, Treasure Hunters, Confessions, Maximum Ride, Witch & Wizard and Daniel X series. James Patterson has been the most borrowed author in UK libraries for the past seven years in a row and his books have sold more than 300 million copies worldwide, making him one of the bestselling authors of all time. He lives in Florida.

JAMES PATTERSON

and CHRIS GRABENSTEIN

ILLUSTRATED BY LAURA PARK

Reissued by Young Arrow in 2015
5 7 9 10 8 6

First published in Great Britain in 2012 by Young Arrow
First published in paperback in Great Britain in 2013 by
Young Arrow
Random House, 20 Vauxhall Bridge Road,
London SW1V 2SA

www.randomhouse.co.uk

Addresses for companies within The Random House Group Limited can
be found at: www.randomhouse.co.uk/offices.htm

The Random House Group Limited Reg. No. 954009

A CIP catalogue record for this book
is available from the British Library

ISBN 9781784750145

The Random House Group Limited supports the Forest Stewardship
Council® (FSC®), the leading international forest-certification organisation.
Our books carrying the FSC label are printed on FSC®-certified paper. FSC is the
only forest-certification scheme supported by the leading environmental
organisations, including Greenpeace. Our paper procurement policy can be
found at www.randomhouse.co.uk/environment

Printed and bound in Great Britain by Clays Ltd, St Ives plc

PROLOGUE

One

FLOP SWEAT

Have you ever done something extremely stupid like, oh, I don't know, try to make a room filled with total strangers laugh until their sides hurt?

Totally dumb, right?

Well, that's why my humble story is going to start with some pretty yucky tension—plus a little heavy-duty drama (and, hopefully, a few funnies so we don't all go nuts).

Okay, so how, exactly, did I get into this mess—up onstage at a comedy club, baking like a bag of French fries under a hot spotlight that shows off my sweat stains (including one that sort of looks like Jabba the Hutt), with about a thousand beady eyeballs drilling into me?

A very good question that you ask.

To tell you the truth, it's one *I'm* asking, too!

What am I, Jamie Grimm, doing here trying to win something called the Planet's Funniest Kid Comic Contest?

What was I thinking?

But wait. Hold on. It gets even worse.

While the whole audience stares and waits for me to say something (anything) funny, I'm up here choking.

That's right—my mind is a *total and complete blank*.

And I just said, "No, I'm Jamie Grimm."

That's the punch line. The *end* of a joke.

All it needs is whatever comes *before* the punch line. You know—all the stuff *I can't remember*.

So I sweat some more. The audience stares some more.

I don't think this is how a comedy act is supposed to go. I'm pretty sure *jokes* are usually involved. And people laughing.

"Um, hi." I finally squeak out a few words. "The other day at school, we had this substitute teacher. Very tough. Sort of like Mrs. Darth

Vader. Had the heavy breathing, the deep voice. During roll call, she said, 'Are you chewing gum, young man?' And I said, 'No, I'm Jamie Grimm.'"

I wait (for what seems like hours) and, yes, the audience kind of chuckles. It's not a huge laugh, but it's a start.

Okay. *Phew*. I can tell a joke. All is not lost. Yet. But hold on for a sec. We need to talk about something else. A major twist to my tale.

"A major twist?" you say. "Already?"

Yep. And, trust me, you weren't expecting this one.

To be totally honest, neither was I.

Two

LADIES AND GENTLEMEN...ME!

Hi.

Presenting me. Jamie Grimm. The sit-down comic.

So, can you deal with this? Some people can. Some can't. Sometimes even *I* can't deal with it (like just about every morning, when I wake up and look at myself in the mirror).

But you know what they say: "If life gives you lemons, learn how to juggle."

Or, even better, learn how to make people laugh.

So that's what I decided to do.

Seriously. I tried to teach myself how to be funny. I did a whole bunch of homework and read every joke book and joke website I could find, just so I could become a comedian and make people laugh.

I guess you could say I'm obsessed with being a stand-up comic—even though I don't exactly fit the job description.

But unlike a lot of homework (algebra, you know I'm talking about *you*), this was fun.

I got to study all the greats: Jon Stewart, Jerry Seinfeld, Kevin James, Ellen DeGeneres, Chris Rock, Steven Wright, Joan Rivers, George Carlin.

I also filled dozens of notebooks with jokes I made up myself—like my second one-liner at the comedy contest.

"Wow, what a crowd," I say, surveying the audience. "Standing room only. Good thing I brought my own chair."

It takes a second, but they laugh—right after I let them know it's okay, because *I'm* smiling, too.

This second laugh? Well, it's definitely bigger than that first chuckle. Who knows—maybe I actually have a shot at winning this thing.

So now I'm not only nervous, I'm *pumped*!

I really, really, *really* (and I mean really) want to take my best shot at becoming the Planet's Funniest Kid Comic.

Because, in a lot of ways, my whole life has been leading up to this one sweet (if sweaty) moment in the spotlight!

PART ONE
The Road to Ronkonkoma

Chapter 1

WELCOME TO MY WORLD

But, hey, I think we're getting ahead of ourselves.

We should probably go back to the beginning—or at least *a* beginning.

So let's check out a typical day in my ordinary, humdrum life in Long Beach, a suburb of New York City—back before my very strange appearance at the Ronkonkoma Comedy Club.

Here's me, just an average kid on an average day in my average house as I open our average door and head off to an average below-average school.

Zombies are *everywhere*.

Well, that's what I see. You might call 'em "ordinary people." To me, these scary people

stumbling down the sidewalks are the living dead!

A pack of brain-numb freaks who crawl out of the ground every morning and shuffle off to work. They're waving at me, grunting "Hul-lo, Ja-mie!" I wave and grunt back.

So what streets do my freaky zombie friends like best? The dead ends, of course.

Fortunately, my neighbors move extremely slowly (lots of foot-dragging and Frankenstein-style lurching). So I never really have to worry about them running me down to scoop out my brains like I'm their personal pudding cup.

There's this one zombie I see almost every morning. He's usually dribbling his coffee and eating a doughnut.

"Do zombies eat doughnuts with their fingers?" you might ask.

No. They usually eat their fingers separately.

The school crossing guard? She can stop traffic just by holding up her hand. With her other hand.

Are there *really* zombies on my way to school every morning?

Of course there are! But only inside my head. Only in my wild imagination. I guess you could say I try to see the funny side of any situation. You should try it sometime. It makes life a lot more interesting.

So how did I end up here in this zombified suburb not too far from New York City?

Well, *that*, my friends, is a very interesting story....

Chapter 2

A STRANGER IN AN EVEN STRANGER LAND

I moved to Long Beach on Long Island only a couple months ago from a small town out in the country. I guess you could say I'm a hick straight from the sticks.

To make my long story a little shorter, Long Beach isn't my home, and I don't think it ever will be. Have you ever felt like you don't fit in? That you don't belong where you are but you're sort of stuck there? Well, that's exactly how I feel each and every day since I moved to Long Beach.

Moving to a brand-new town also means I have to face a brand-new bunch of kids, and bullies, at my brand-new school.

Now, like all the other schools I've ever attended, the hallways of Long Beach Middle School are plastered with all sorts of NO BULLYING posters. There's only one problem: Bullies, it turns out, don't read too much. I guess reading really isn't a job requirement in the high-paying fields of name-calling, nose-punching, and atomic-wedgie-yanking.

You want to know the secret to not getting beat up at school?

Well, I don't really have scientific proof or anything, but, in my experience, comedy works. Most of the time, anyway.

That's right: Never underestimate the power of a good laugh. It can stop some of the fiercest middle-school monsters.

For instance, if you hit your local bully with a pretty good joke, he or she might be too busy laughing to hit you back. It's true: Punch lines can actually beat punches because it's pretty hard for a bully to give you a triple nipple cripple if he's doubled over, holding his sides, and laughing his head off.

So every morning, before heading off to school, just make sure you pack some good jokes along with your lunch. For instance, you could distract your bully with a one-liner from one of my all-time favorite stand-up comics, Steven Wright: "Do you think that when they asked George Washington for ID, he just whipped out a quarter?"

If that doesn't work, go with some surefire Homer Simpson: "Operator! Give me the number for 9-1-1!"

All I'm saying is that laughing is healthy. A lot healthier than getting socked in the stomach. Especially if you had a big breakfast.

Chapter 3

JAMIE TO THE RESCUE!

Of course, my new school gives me all sorts of terrific opportunities to test my "anti-bullying" theories.

Because once I make it through my Imaginary Zombie Zone, there's another drooling demon for me to deal with. A *real* one.

Meet Stevie Kosgrov. Long Beach's Bully of the Year, three years running. All-Pro. Master of Disaster. Inventor of the Upside-Down Shanghai Shakedown. Kosgrov puts the cruel in Long Beach Middle School.

As I cruise across the playground, he's busy making change with a sixth grader and gravity. The poor kid's in serious trouble. I know because I've been in his position before: upside down, with loose change sprinkling out of my pockets.

I roll right up to Kosgrov and his victim.

Inside, I'm trembling. Outside, I try not to let it show. Bullies can smell fear. Sweat, too. They're also pretty good at picking up on involuntary toots.

"Hey, Stevie," I say as calmly and coolly as I can. "How's it going?"

"Get lost, Grimm. I'm busy here."

"Sure. Say, did you hear about the kidnapping?"

"No."

"Don't worry. He woke up."

The upside-down kid losing all his lunch money laughs at the joke. Stevie does not.

"And how about that karate champion who joined the army?"

"What about him?"

"Oh, I hear it was pretty bad. First time he saluted, he nearly killed himself."

Kosgrov's victim is totally cracking up. Kosgrov? Not so much.

Desperate, I try one more time with what I think is some can't-miss Homer Simpson material: "Yesterday I asked my teacher, 'How come I have to study English? I'm never going to England!'"

Stevie still isn't laughing, but he does, finally, loosen his grip on the small kid's ankles.

The little guy drops to the ground—and takes off like a race car at Talladega Superspeedway.

"Thanks, Jamie! I owe you one!" I think that's what he says. He's running away very, very quickly when he says it.

Meanwhile, Kosgrov redirects his rage. At me.

He lurches forward, grabs hold of both my armrests, and leans down. I'm basically frozen in place. Petrifying fear and locked wheel brakes will do that to you.

From his hot, steamy breath, I can tell that Stevie Kosgrov recently enjoyed a bowl of Fruity Pebbles (with milk that had hit its expiration date, oh, maybe a month ago).

"What?" says Kosgrov. "You think I won't lay you out just because you're stuck in a wheelchair, funny boy?"

"Yeah," I say. "Pretty much."

Turns out I'm pretty wrong.

Chapter 7

DOWN AND UP

This is so awesome!

Kosgrov decks me. I mean, he socks me so hard I end up flat on my back like a tipped-over turtle (minus the kicking legs). I'm down for the count—well, I would be if Kosgrov could count. He's about as good at math as he is at reading.

Lying on the ground, staring up at the sky with parking-lot gravel in my hair, I feel that I have finally arrived.

Birdie, birdie in the sky, why'd you do that in my eye?

GET UP, YA BUM!

Stevie Kosgrov punched me just like I was a *regular, normal kid.*

He didn't call me gimp or crip or Wheelie McFeelie. He just slugged me in the gut and laughed hysterically when I toppled backward. He even kicked my wheelchair off to the side so I'd look more like an average loser sprawled out on the black asphalt.

This is progress.

The world just became a little better place.

I'm not the kid in the wheelchair anymore (and not just because Stevie knocked me out of it). I feel normal, and normal feels absolutely amazing.

You see, once you've been labeled a "special needs" kid, being "ordinary," even if it's being ordinary sprawled out flat on your back, is the most incredible feeling in the world.

So, thank you, Stevie Kosgrov!

I can see why you, sir, are the champ. You bully without regard to race, religion, creed, national origin, or physical abilities. You are an equal-opportunity tormentor.

Fortunately, my two best friends, Pierce and Gaynor, come along and help me back into my chair.

They're both supercool. Good peeps.

"Hey, guys," I say. "Did I beat the count? I want a rematch! I was robbed. Where's Kosgrov? Let me at 'im! Yo, Adrian? We did it! Adrian!!!!"

Yeah, I'm a huge *Rocky* fan. I liked *Real Steel*, too. And *The Champ*.

"Are you okay, Jamie?" asks Pierce.

"Never better. Was that great or what?"

"Seriously. Come on, Jamie. Quit goofing around."

"I'm fine," I say. "Nothing is broken—that wasn't broken before."

"You're sure?"

"Positive. I wouldn't lie to you guys."

We head into school. Pierce and Gaynor don't grab hold of the chair's handles to push me like I'm a baby in a stroller. They just walk beside me—like wingmen.

Like I'm a normal bud.

I think somebody once said that friends are the family we choose.

You don't know how lucky I am that Pierce and Gaynor chose me. These two guys are awesome. The best.

Chapter 5

AND NOW—THE GOOD STUFF

You look at me, and I know what you're thinking: "Zac Efron without the hot legs."

Okay. Maybe not. But I do have a pretty good set of guns. Check out my bulging biceps. Those mosquito-bite bumps on my arms there.

Girls look at me and think, "Oooh. Take me to the mall or the movies or Taco Bell!" They probably figure we can park in a handicapped space close to the doors.

Now, I'm guessing you go to school, too. So you know what that's like. All the bad stuff, like rubbery pizza in the cafeteria and pop quizzes in social studies, and let's not even get into that sawdusty stuff the janitor sprinkles over the occasional puke puddle.

So let me just tell you the *good* parts about my school.

There's cold chocolate milk in the cafeteria. *Every day!*

And, of course, I've got my two best buds. You already met them—Pierce and Gaynor. Pierce is a total brainiac. He can tell you everything you ever wanted to know, like how you mark a baseball scorecard with a backward *K* for a called third strike and a forward *K* if the batter strikes out swinging.

Gaynor is a little more edgy. A little more "out there," if you know what I mean. He actually has tattoos and a nose ring.

30

I don't think I'll ever get a tattoo. With my luck, the guy working the ink needle would get the hiccups and I'd end up with a squiggly butterfly instead of a fire-breathing dragon.

My friends are both excellent squatters. When I started using the chair, the whole world seemed to grow three feet taller, and everybody was always looking down on me. Literally. But not Gaynor and Pierce.

If we're just hanging out, they'll both hunker down into a deep knee bend or find something to sit on so we're all talking eye to eye. They're not just thinking about themselves; they're thinking about me, too.

Anyway, another good thing about my school? The science lab. If you stare out the third window just the right way, you get an excellent view of the ocean and the beach. Well, it's only a tiny sliver, but if you squint real hard, you can see the surf *and* my Uncle Frankie's diner.

Then there's this frizzy-haired girl who's in a couple of my classes. She's definitely another good thing about school. She laughed once in math class when I cracked a joke about parallel lines: "When all those parallel lines finally meet in infinity, do they throw a party?"

The frizzy-haired girl has a very bubbly laugh.

She's also extremely cute. But who am I kidding? She probably doesn't even know I exist. I'm just the jokester sitting in the back of the classroom. Other than that, I'm totally invisible to her. Which reminds me of this awful joke (what I call a "groaner") that I read in one of my giant jokelopedias:

A nurse goes into a doctor's office and says, "Doctor, there's a man out here who thinks he's invisible."

"I'm busy," says the doctor. "Tell him I can't see him right now."

Pretty corny, huh? But I figure the frizzy-haired girl feels the same way about me.

That I'm invisible.

I guess all the cute girls do.

I also have a feeling they always will.

Chapter 6

MY AFTER-SCHOOL SPECIAL

The final bell rings at school, and I'm off like a shot.

I'm the first one out of the building every afternoon.

I zip down the sidewalk and head to my Uncle Frankie's diner. I love spending time with Frankie.

He owns the oldest diner in the whole New York metropolitan area. It's so old, I think when it opened, Burger King was still a prince.

Even the jukebox plays nothing but oldies, mostly doo-wop tunes from the 1950s and '60s. Uncle Frankie isn't just the owner; he's also the head chef.

And, get this: He's the former yo-yo champion of all of Brooklyn, a place famous for its yo-yos. Uncle Frankie is always doing yo-yo tricks, even when he's working the grill. He can Hop the Fence, Walk the Dog, Loop the Loop, and go Around the World with one hand while flipping griddle cakes and two eggs over easy with the other.

"So how was school today, Jamie?" he asks once I'm parked in the kitchen.

"Not bad. I took out a bully today."

"Really?"

"Yeah. He was picking on this sixth grader, so I pulled a Chuck Norris and did what needed to be done."

"You stood up for this other kid?"

"Well, I didn't exactly *stand*."

"You know what I mean."

"Yeah. I do."

Uncle Frankie puts down his yo-yo and nods proudly. "You did good, Jamie."

"Well, you know what Kevin James says in *Mall Cop*: If—"

Frankie holds up a hand. "No joke, kiddo. I'm proud of you. Seriously proud."

"Thanks." I'm sort of blushing when I say it.

Neither one of us says anything else for a while. The only sound in the kitchen is grease sputtering on the grill and some plates clanking behind us.

I don't do so well with long, thoughtful pauses or total quiet. Gives me a little too much time to think about my situation and how absolutely alone I sometimes feel.

So I rev up my motor mouth.

"Oh, and this morning, on my way to school? I wiped out a whole bunch of zombies. Rolled over them, too. I may never get all the green slime out of my tire treads."

"Is that so?" says Uncle Frankie, shaking his head and smiling. "Zombies?"

"Yep," I say. "All in all, it was just your average, ho-hum kind of day."

"So, Jamie—you ever think about writing down your wacky stories so you can tell them to people in a comedy club or something?"

I shrug. "Sometimes. Maybe. Not really."

"You should. You crack me up, kiddo. You'd crack up other people, too. Trust me on this one. I know a little something about show business."

"Because you were a yo-yo champion?"

"Exactly! I've been on the big stage, and it's very cool."

So, as they say—maybe in Iowa or Nebraska—the seed was planted.

chapter 7

THERE'S NO PLACE LIKE HOME (IF THERE WERE, THE AUTHORITIES WOULD SHUT IT DOWN)

After a healthy after-school snack of French fries and ketchup (they're both, technically, vegetables), it's time to leave the diner and head for home, a little place I call "Smileyville."

I moved to Long Beach when my mother's sister (we'll call her Aunt Smiley) adopted me. Yes, I wish my father's brother, Uncle Frankie, had adopted me, but the judge sent me to Smileyville instead.

I'm not sure my mother's sister was all that excited about adding me to her family. Have you ever seen one of those ADOPT A HIGHWAY signs on the interstate? I think that would've been her first choice.

The Smileys are the most clueless, absentminded people you'll ever meet. They hardly notice I'm around—which basically works in my favor because I can sneak out pretty easily.

But the most important thing about my adoptive family is that I call them "the Smileys" because they *never, ever* smile.

You could bring home ice cream and cupcakes, and these people would still pout. You could pop open a crate full of adorable, tail-wagging puppies, and they wouldn't even crack a grin.

In fact, they already have a dog. I call him "Ol' Smiler." Look up "hangdog expression" in the dictionary, and you'll see his face.

There's only one good thing about being adopted by a family that never, ever smiles: They're the perfect test audience for my jokes. If I can make *these* people laugh, I'm pretty sure I can make *anybody* laugh.

Oh, there's one tiny thing that makes living in Smileyville even worse.

Yep. It's time for another curveball.

Chapter 8

WITH BROTHERS LIKE THIS, WHO NEEDS ENEMIES?

Meet my brand-new big brother.
And by *big*, I mean HUGE.

You are correct. It's Stevie Kosgrov. The same bully who made my day by knocking me out of my wheelchair.

Officially, he is now my adoptive brother because Aunt Smiley is Stevie's mom.

As you might imagine, living with my new adoptive brother is a lot less *Brady Bunch* and much more *Harry Potter*. Stevie Kosgrov is my very own somewhat demented Dudley Dursley— if Dudley had muscles and serious BO issues and knew how to jam people's heads down toilets to give them a swirly.

Yes, Stevie Kosgrov makes my new home a living hell. Except for the heat.

My new bedroom is so cold, last night I saw a spider in the corner standing on one leg.

Sorry. Those are David Letterman jokes, and David Letterman is one of my idols.

Chapter 9

BRAINSTORMING!

Every night after dinner—which is usually something like tuna noodle casserole made with cream-of-wallpaper soup—I escape to the privacy of my bedroom.

Actually, it used to be the garage, which probably explains why it's never what you might call warm or toasty.

"That's where we keep all the crap with wheels," Stevie said the day I moved in. "The lawn mower, the snowblower, and *you*!"

In fairness, Uncle Smiley cleaned the place out. He even put rugs over all the oil and antifreeze splotches on the floor.

The *cold* concrete floor.

On the plus side, I'm the only kid I know with a genuine Weedwacker hanging on his wall.

Could you keep it down? I'm trying to work!

My bedroom is also where I keep my massive collection of joke books and notebooks. Whenever I have an idea for a comic sketch or bit, I roll in here, grab a notebook and a pen, and go to work.

For instance, last night the Smileys were watching that National Geographic movie *March of the Penguins*. It's their kind of movie. Lots of ice, blizzards, gale-force winds, and those cute little penguins everywhere.

By the way, did you know that penguins mate for life? Then again, they all look the same, so how do they even know if their girlfriend is really *their* girlfriend?

See, this is what I do.

I brainstorm every silly angle I can think of on a subject, jot it all down (no judgments allowed during brainstorming), and then try to work it into a bit.

Maybe I could do a riff on this penguin stand-up comic I pretend I know. Poor guy, all he can tell are black-and-white jokes. "What's black

and white and black and white and black and white? A nun in a revolving door. Or me. In a revolving door. Or my mother. In a..."

I'm working away, thinking about what Uncle Frankie said, the seed he planted, when all of a sudden there's this terrible banging on my bedroom door.

"Whatcha doin' in there, Jamie?"

It's Stevie Kosgrov, my adoptive brother.

My escape into my imaginary world is cut short by his very *real* pounding and howling.

I don't feel so funny when Stevie's knocking on my bedroom door. To be honest, I feel trapped.

Which, I guess, I kind of am.

IT'S A SMALL BEACH, AFTER ALL

The next day, thank goodness, is Saturday. To once again quote the great Homer Simpson: "Woo-hoo!"

Time to roll up the garage door, say good-bye to Smileyville, and breeze down to the Long Beach boardwalk, which is about a mile shorter than the long beach that Long Beach is named after—two and a quarter miles. Uncle Frankie tells me it was built back in 1914—with the help of elephants.

Yep. It's already in one of my notebooks. A bit about elephants trying to figure out how to hold a hammer, since they don't have any thumbs. Then I say, "No one really cared how long it took for

the elephants to
hammer in a nail.
They worked for peanuts."

Okay. That one still needs a little tweaking. I'll
work on it.

What I like best about the beach and
boardwalk is all the different kinds of people I
see. Russian grandmas in head scarves. Hispanic
families eating rainbow-colored snow cones.
Hasidic men with curly side locks and big hats.
Koreans and Chinese smiling in the sunshine.
Italians with lots of back hair. Irish with lots of
freckles every place the Italians have hair.

Maybe they should call this United Nations
Beach.

Okay. I'm pulling out my notebook to jot this down. It could be a whole new bit for my act.

Sand, sun, and surf—the great equalizers. Proof that people everywhere can get along in peace and harmony, as long as none of them play their music too loud and everybody remembers to use sunblock.

On United Nations Beach, there are no borders. Just blankets.

And everybody looks basically the same in a bathing suit. Especially old guys in Speedos. They all look ridiculous.

But wait—this is bigger than every country in the world.

I see fat people, skinny people, workout freaks, hipsters, bankers (who else would wear a suit to the beach?). I see zombies playing Frisbee with penguins. Penguins wearing black-and-white bikinis.

What if life really were a beach?

What if the sun shone every day, and all you had to do all day was splash in the surf, boogie board, apply sunblock, and spear a couple of sand crabs for dinner?

Maybe this is the secret to world peace?

Make everybody everywhere move to the nearest beach.

There would be no more wars—just a few small action-figure skirmishes around sand castles.

Of course, I do have one absolutely horrible fear about the beach.

Turn the page...if you dare.

Chapter 11

SAND TRAPPED

My problem? My great fear? Think about it from my perspective.

The beach is made out of sand. My wheelchair only comes with two-wheel drive, and it sure isn't a dune buggy. See where I'm going with this? Of course you do.

I wouldn't be able to budge. I'd sink.

I'd be like Han, Leia, and Luke in *Star Wars: Return of the Jedi*. Stuck on the endless expanse of the Tatooine desert—waiting for some sand creature to come along and suck me down into its sand pit for dinner, or maybe just a snack.

To me, the beach is just a desert surrounded by water you can't drink!

I'd be stranded in my wheelchair as it slowly sank deeper and deeper.

No water. No sunblock.

I...can't...go...on...

Ack!

It'd be horrible.

Plus, I'd have sand in my socks. Probably my underpants, too.

THERE'S NOTHING FINER THAN SATURDAY AT THE DINER

Next stop?

Up the boardwalk a couple of blocks to Frankie's Good Eats by the Sea. My uncle's diner is always packed on Saturdays, so sometimes I lend a hand, helping out behind the cash register.

The best part? I get to tell a joke to every single person I ring up.

"Here's your change, Mrs. P.—and how about a little Rodney Dangerfield for dessert?"

The woman smiles. She's a real sweetheart. "Okay."

I tug at my collar, like Rodney would. "I tell you, I come from a stupid family. During the Civil War, my great-uncle fought for the *West*!"

Mrs. P. cracks up. The next guy steps up to my register and hands me his guest check. He's one of my regulars, Mr. Emilito. Delivers newspapers house to house.

I tell ya, when I was a kid, all I knew was rejection. My yo-yo? It never came back.

Badda-bing!

* Another classic Rodney Dangerfield joke.

"What've you got for me, Jamie? Make me laugh."

I make his change first. "Fifty-three cents and some classic George Carlin."

"Excellent!"

"Can vegetarians eat animal crackers? Hey, how do they get the deer to cross at that yellow road sign? I put a dollar in a change machine. Nothing changed."

He's laughing so hard, he almost swallows his toothpick.

So I work in a little of my own material.

"If number two pencils are so popular, why are they still number two?"

Mr. Emilito is still cracking up. "Who does that one?" he asks. "Carlin?"

"Nope. That one's mine."

"Really? Awesome!"

And he tosses his fifty-three cents into the tip cup that Uncle Frankie keeps on the counter.

Wow. I think I just became a professional comedian.

"You know," says Uncle Frankie, "you've got a gift, Jamie."

"Really? Did it come with a gift receipt? Because I've had my eye on an iPod...."

"Jamie? Can you maybe be serious for two seconds?"

"I can try."

"Good. I saw this in the paper. You should enter this comedy contest. Think about it. I've seen you with the customers, kiddo. And with Joey Gaynor and Jimmy Pierce," says Uncle Frankie. "You're hysterical. You could win. Seriously."

I disagree. Seriously.

One, I don't think I'm funny enough. Not even close.

Two, I'd definitely choke.

Because I'm a choker.

Seriously.

FROM RUSSIA, WITH LOVE

Later at the diner, I ring up another regular, an old man named Mr. Burdzecki.

He's Russian. So I dig deep and pull out some classic Yakov Smirnoff from all the way back in the 1980s. Like, another *century*.

"Did you see the ad in the paper this morning, Mr. Burdzecki? It said 'Big Sale. Last Week.' Last week? Why advertise? I already missed it. They're just rubbing it in."

He laughs. Like a happy bear.

So I keep going.

"Yakov Smirnoff says that in Russia, there were only two TV channels. Channel One was propaganda. Channel Two was a KGB officer telling you, 'Turn back to Channel One.'"

Mr. Burdzecki is drying his eyes with a paper napkin. He's a really nice man.

"You funny boy," he says.

"I funny?"

"*Da*. You funny."

Okay. If he says so.

I funny!

Chapter 14

THERE'S NO PLACE LIKE HOME (SERIOUSLY, THERE ISN'T)

Unfortunately, my day at the diner ends, and I have to head for home.

Well, it's not really home. I guess I don't really have a home anymore. Before I came to Long Beach I lived in a small town called Cornwall, where life was definitely good. Tall mountains. Deep blue lakes. Forests that went on forever.

I used to love to go exploring. I'd imagine stories, like I was Captain Jack Sparrow and the woods were my pirate hideout. Other times I'd be the Master Chief and tear through the forest, pretending it was filled with all the alien creatures from *Halo*.

I'd give anything to go back to the way things used to be. But I can't. I guess none of us ever can, right?

So what happened to make me move to Long Beach? And live with the Smileys?

Nothing I really want to talk about. And I *definitely* don't want to bore you with the details about how I ended up in this wheelchair.

Like I said, it's not really worth it.

In fact, it's a total buzzkill.

So, you know—'nuff said.

Chapter 15

HOME IS WHERE THE HEARTLESS BULLY IS

On the way home, I'm thinking about what Uncle Frankie said about that funny-kid contest. And I'm still in the same place: *No way. I'd choke!*

When I finally reach Smileyville, I notice that the family's road-hogging, gas-guzzling, DVD-playing SUV is gone.

So are the Smileys.

So I reach into my backpack, fish around inside, and find the remote-control garage door opener.

I know. Most kids have a set of house keys. I have a Genie garage door opener from Home Depot.

It's okay. I'm fine with it. Home sweet garage.

I aim the remote at the door and wait for the

familiar click, whir, and grind of the slowly rising paneled door.

Only it doesn't come.

So I aim and fire again. I also notice that since the sun went down about fifteen minutes earlier, the temperature has plunged, like, twenty degrees. My bedroom may be chilly, but at least it's warmer than the driveway.

I thumb the remote a third time.

The garage door still doesn't budge. So, like most guys, I keep pointing and clicking—thinking that if I stun the door opener with just enough infrared beams, it will magically remember how to work.

That's when I hear laughter. Actually, it's more like howling.

Stevie is in the living room, leering down at me like a lunatic. He looks like a big baboon who's angry because the zookeepers won't toss him any more bananas. He is also laughing like a hyena.

"What's the matter, Jamie?" he shouts through the glass. "Somebody unplug your door opener?"

"Let me in, Stevie."

"Not gonna happen, stepbro."

"C'mon."

"What? You think you're special? Use the front door, like everybody else."

Now he laughs even harder.

I would go around to the door on the side of the garage, but Uncle Smiley dead-bolted it shut "for security purposes" when I moved in. He also didn't give me a key. (Have I mentioned how clueless my adoptive parents are? I did? Good. Just checking.)

Meanwhile, the temperature keeps dropping.

"Have a nice night, bro!" Stevie cries from the window. And then he disappears.

Leaving me to freeze in peace.

Great. I've always loved Popsicles. I just never wanted to turn into one.

ME AND MY CRAZY FRIENDS

Yes, the other Smileys finally came home and, yes, my body finally thawed out.

(Now I know how a bag of frozen broccoli feels.)

On Monday morning it's back-to-school time, which is fine by me. School means I get to hang with my friends, at least.

I meet up with Pierce and Gaynor in the schoolyard.

Pierce is so smart, he could probably teach the teachers.

"Did you know," he says, "that the average life span of a major-league baseball is seven pitches?"

"No," I say. "I did not know that."

"It's true. And it's rumored that Coca-Cola was originally green."

After Pierce hits me with a few fun facts, I try to return the favor with a fresh math joke.

"So how come calculus and girls are the same?"

"I dunno," says Pierce. "How come?"

"Because I don't understand either one."

"Speaking of girls..." says Gaynor.

Have I mentioned that Gaynor is girl-crazy? I think the nose ring short-circuited something in his brain. All he ever wants to talk about is girls. Probably because he's afraid to talk *to* them.

(Aren't we all? Well, probably not if you're a girl, but...oh, never mind.)

"I'm thinking about getting Suzie Orolvsky's name tattooed on my knuckles," Gaynor announces.

"Who's she?" I ask.

"That girl in physics," says Pierce. "You know, Jamie. The one *you're* always gawking at."

I don't know who, or what, he's talking about.

"So what do you guys think?" says Gaynor, holding up both his fists. "I could put one letter on each finger."

"Bad idea," I say. "Everybody will think you're in love with S-U-Z-I-E-O-R-O."

Gaynor gets it finally. "Oh, man. I need to fall in love with a girl who has a way shorter name. Like Meg Choo. She's cool."

Like I said, Gaynor is girl-crazy. Or maybe he's just plain wacko. Either way, I love the guy.

I'm tempted to ask my friends what they think of Uncle Frankie's idea—me trying out for the funny-kid contest.

But I don't ask.

Know why?

Because I *choke* on the words.

THE BIGGEST LOSER

By now you know I love to tell jokes.

But other people, it seems, love to *play* jokes. Especially on me.

This is why I have such a terrible time at school that day. Maybe the worst since I got to Long Beach.

Those two jokesters Pierce and Gaynor somehow managed to get my name on the student council ballot. There's a check box next to it and everything. So now I'm officially running to be a class representative.

They even made posters—and hung them in the halls!

Yes, my total humiliation has gone totally public.

"Why would you guys do something so dumb?" I ask them when we meet up again in the cafeteria for lunch.

"Dumb?" says Pierce. "Bull! You're the best man for the job, Jamie."

"I am not."

"Yeah, you are," says Gaynor. "You're honest. You say what you mean. You've got guts."

"Jamie," says Pierce, "the student council would be lucky to have you. You have an excellent sense of humor, which can be useful during heated debates."

Wow. Maybe my two best friends were serious about me running for office. That made me feel pretty good, actually. For, like, four hours.

Until the announcements at the end of the day. They read the election results.

I got three votes. Three out of three hundred sixty-one.

I know Gaynor and Pierce voted for me, but I can't figure out who the third vote came from. The only thing I know for sure is it wasn't me! I swear—I did not vote for myself.

In fact, I voted for a write-in candidate. Bart Simpson. Now, *he's* funny. Bart Simpson would be great on the student council. Bart Simpson could be the Planet's Funniest Kid Comic, too.

It's definitely not me.

Chapter 18

THE CRIP FROM CORNBALL

The funny thing is, I used to be ready to try anything. I had no fear. Maybe I should have, though.

Like I said, I used to live in a small town called Cornwall in upstate New York. Well, that's what people who live there call it. And the people who make maps.

Stevie Kosgrov? He calls it "Cornball." Making me the "crip from Cornball."

Seems before I moved to Smileyville, Stevie had his eye on the garage.

"I wanted that to be *my* bedroom," he says. "It'd be so easy to sneak out at night to TP yards, egg cars, and punch people." Yes, Stevie has an active social life.

He also shadows me wherever I go. School.
The bathroom. The movies.

"And don't think I won't punch you!" he's
always saying.

"You already *did* punch me!" I want to remind
him, but I never do, because it might make him
mad enough to punch me again.

"I'll punch anybody and anything!" he boasts.
"Girls, old people, fire hydrants, even goldfish."

Yes, Stevie Kosgrov claims he actually
punched out a goldfish once.

When he was a baby. With teeny-tiny fists.

"I didn't like the way the thing was looking at me with that sideways eyeball. So I smacked it right in the kisser."

And unlike the miniature snack crackers, this goldfish did *not* smile back.

MY LUNCH DATE

The next day at lunch, I make my way to our usual table in the far corner of the cafeteria and discover that Pierce and Gaynor have invited someone new to join our crew.

The girl with the frizzy hair.

"Hey, Jamie," says Gaynor. "You know Gilda Gold, right? From math class? She's a girl."

"Gilda's in my robotics club," adds Pierce. "She told me she likes those jokes you crack all the time from the back of the room. So I invited her to join us for lunch so she could officially meet you."

I'm nodding, staring, and saying something like, "Stammer, stammer, stammer, stammer."

Or maybe it's "Hummina, hummina, hummina," which is what the old-time TV comedian Jackie Gleason used to jabber whenever he choked.

Whatever I do, it makes Gilda giggle. She thinks I'm trying to be funny.

"I bet you say that to all the girls," she says, giving me her bubbly laugh.

Which gives me enough confidence to get out, "Usually I say something like, 'Haven't I seen you someplace before?' And then they say, 'Yeah, that's why I don't go there anymore.'"

Gilda laughs and then flings me her own comeback joke: "Yesterday this total jerk actually asked me what my sign was. I told him, 'No Parking.'"

Now it's my turn to laugh, and suddenly it's like we have this whole history between us, even though we don't. Just math class. And a love of jokes, I guess.

Gaynor and Pierce slide down to the end of the table to play flick football.

Gilda Gold and I crack open our chocolate-milk cartons and talk like crazy. She tells me how she

moved to Long Beach from New England. I tell
her a little bit about Cornwall. She loves baseball,
especially the Boston Red Sox, even though
wearing a BoSox hat is lethally dangerous this
close to New York City. (Long Beach is diehard
Yankees territory.) I tell her how I used to love
playing baseball. Center field. Then I realize what
I'm getting into—and I stop myself.

"Now I mostly play DVDs of old movies," I say.

"I *love* old movies!" Gilda gushes. "Comedies?"

"Definitely. *Blazing Saddles* and *Airplane!* and
anything with Will Ferrell. What about the Marx
Brothers?" I ask.

"I *love* those guys!"

I pick up my milk straw and start doing
my best Groucho impersonation. "Hello, room
service? Send up a larger room."

Gilda giggles. I keep going.

"Outside of a dog, a book is man's best friend.
Inside of a dog, it's too dark to read."

And that's when Stevie Kosgrov shows up.

His fist has some kind of brown goop smeared
on it. I think he just punched somebody's bean
burrito.

"Why you wearing that hat?" he says to Gilda.

"Um, because I like the Sox."

Kosgrov cocks back his arm. "Consider this a warning, sister. You better watch yourself."

"Okay. Sure." Gilda pulls out her makeup mirror. Stares at her reflection. "I'm watching myself."

When Kosgrov stomps away, it's Gilda's turn to quote some Groucho to me: "He may look like an idiot and talk like an idiot, but don't let that fool you. He really is an idiot."

Yep. She funny.

Chapter 20

WHY "PUBLIC SPEAKING" SHOULD BE CALLED "PUBLIC EXECUTION"

I wish I could say that after lunch with Gilda and the guys, my day just kept getting better and better.

I guess if this were a Hollywood movie, that's how things would go. Unfortunately, it's just my life.

Right after lunch, I have ELA. English Language Arts. One of those arts, I hate to say, is public speaking.

And it's my turn to give a speech.

I chose the topic "Climbing Mount Everest."

Why not? Fiction is one of the language arts,
too.

"Today," I say when I'm in front of everybody,
"I'd like to talk to you about climbing Mount
Everest—the mountain, which Tibetans call
Jomolungma, a name that means 'Holy Mother.'

"And that's exactly what I said the first time
I saw the summit looming in the distance: 'Holy
Mother, what have I gotten myself into this
time?'"

The class and Mrs. Kanai, our teacher, laugh.

"But it had always been my dream to reach
the Top of the World, as Everest, the highest

mountain peak on earth, is sometimes called. However, I had been hoping that Donald Trump would just drop me off in one of his helicopters. But it wasn't meant to be. The Donald was busy making another couple of billions that day.

"'Why Everest?' you may ask. 'Because it's there' is the most famous answer. 'There was nothing good on TV' is another."

More laughs.

"And so with my trusted Sherpa guide and a sled dog named Bob, I set out from Kathmandu.

"We made our way to base camp and spent two weeks adjusting to the higher altitude and lack of oxygen. We all sounded like we'd been sucking helium out of birthday balloons.

"Finally, we set out for the summit. Yes, it was hard. Yes, it was dangerous. Yes, we had to wear helmets that gave us horrible hat hair, but it was worth it. Because I knew that if I could ascend Mount Everest, I would show the world that I could overcome any obstacle life put in my way. I could achieve any dream I dreamed. And so I pushed myself. Literally. I mean I used both arms and *pushed*—hard. That Everest is *steep*.

"Suddenly, an unexpected storm erupted. Thunder boomed. Snow swirled all around me. My wheels became caked with ice. My spokes became icicles. My Sherpa guide and Bob the sled dog both said we should turn back. But I said no! I could see the summit! I could..."

Actually, what I see are two dozen pairs of eyeballs staring at me. My audience is dying to hear how my story ends.

And then a real storm erupts. A sweat storm. My armpits look like I've been popping water balloons down there. I can't remember how the speech is supposed to end.

All of a sudden, I have a new dream: to disappear right into the floor!

Chapter 21

FIRST AID FOR CHOKING VICTIMS

Totally embarrassed, I bolt out of school before the final bell even stops ringing.

I don't hang out with Pierce and Gaynor. I don't say good-bye to Gilda. I just roll my sweaty butt down the boardwalk to Uncle Frankie's diner.

"So how was your day?" he asks.

"Terrible. This morning, when I put on my underwear, I could hear the Fruit of the Loom guys laughing at me."

"Jamie?"

"Yeah?"

"That's a Rodney Dangerfield joke. You told it last weekend to Mrs. Nicolo. I'm asking about *your* day, not Mr. Dangerfield's."

"It was horrible. I choked."

"Did you try the Heimlich maneuver?" cracks Uncle Frankie.

It makes me smile. "That's pretty good," I say. "I may steal it."

"Be my guest. Anything I can do to help."

I sigh and get serious. "Today in ELA, I had to give a speech, and it was going pretty good right up to when it wasn't. I panicked, Uncle Frankie. My mind went totally and completely blank. I choked."

Uncle Frankie gives me a knowing nod, like he's been there, done that.

"You know, Jamie, I read this magazine article once. It said the fear of public speaking is second—only to the fear of death—in the dread-and-anxiety department."

"I guess that's why comedians say they're 'dying' when nobody laughs at their jokes."

"Whoa. Hold on, kiddo. *Everybody* laughs at your jokes. I've heard 'em."

"Only if I don't freeze up first. Like, if there was a little pressure on me. Or an audience of more than one or two."

"So allow me to pass along some advice a customer—a guy who teaches public speaking at City College—told me once. He said everybody gets stage fright. The key to beating it is practicing the three Ps."

"You're saying I should do more bathroom humor?"

"Jamie?"

"Sorry."

"Practice. Prepare. Perform."

I nod.

"Hang on a second," says Uncle Frankie. He goes to this drawer where he keeps junk, like the halves of broken yo-yos and extra spools of yo-yo string. "This speech teacher—he gave me a pamphlet for a seminar he leads." He hands me the slim brochure. "Take it home, Jamie."

"Great. Now even my favorite uncle is giving me homework."

"Only because I love you, kiddo."

I smile when he says that. "Yeah. I know."

THE LONG WAY HOME

After visiting the diner (and helping out behind the cash register during the dinner rush), I take the long way back to Smileyville.

I'm not in that big of a hurry to head for "home."

Plus, the boardwalk is incredibly beautiful after the sun goes down. It's just me and the stars and the ocean crashing against the shore.

Very peaceful.

I love the beach and the boardwalk—almost as much as I loved my old life back in Cornwall.

Almost.

Yeah, I miss Cornwall like crazy.

What exactly do I miss so much?

Everything. And everybody. I miss the way things used to be, you know?

The people who used to be in my life.

The people who used to be my life.

Sorry. That's all I can give you right now. The beach, especially at night, is a total No Buzzkill zone.

Chapter 23

A BAD DREAM COME TRUE

Speaking of a totally incredible buzzkill...

Who should come bopping up the boardwalk but Stevie Kosgrov and a couple of his creepy friends—guys he probably met while doing hard time in detention hall.

"Well, if it isn't the crip from Cornball." Stevie sneers as he and his two pals block my way forward.

When I try to back up, one of the knuckle-dragging thugs grabs hold of a railing, swings around, and ends up behind me.

I'm totally surrounded. It's like a bully doughnut, and I'm the squishy jelly in the middle.

"Where you going, funny boy?" Stevie asks.

"Home," I mumble.

"You mean Cornball? Then I think you're heading in the wrong direction."

He grabs my armrests and spins me around. Then he tilts me backward till I'm staring straight up at the sky.

"You know, Forrest Gimp, you should do like sailors do when they're lost: Follow the stars! Can you see the stars, Jamie?"

I don't know why exactly, but I crack wise in reply: "You mean those tiny twinkling things up in the sky? I always wondered what those were called." And then I follow up with an insult joke. "Stevie, you ate paint chips in your crib—am I right?"

"Are you mouthing off to me?"

"No. I was just—"

He doesn't wait for my next snappy comeback. He dumps me. He lets go of my handles and lets me fall backward and hit the deck, hard. So hard, I actually see a few *more* stars.

"Grab his chair, Zits," Stevie says to one of his hoodlum friends.

"Got it."

"Yo," he calls to the other goon. "Give me a hand, Useless. It's time to toss out the trash."

Stevie grabs my arms. Zits and Useless grab my legs. They start swinging me back and forth like I'm a hammock somebody hung up in a hurricane.

"One...two..."

I close my eyes. *This is really bad. Even for Stevie, this is over the top.*

"Three!"

They heave me up and over the railing. I sail about ten yards and hit the sand with a hard thud.

"Let's get out of here!" I hear Stevie holler.

Then he and his two buddies—all of them laughing hysterically—take off down the boardwalk, pushing my wheelchair like they're in some kind of shopping-cart race.

My nightmare of nightmares has come true. I am officially stranded in the sand.

But there's no way I am yelling for help. How embarrassing would that be? "Um, excuse me, I seem to have lost my wheelchair. Would you mind dragging me off this beach before an army of sand crabs invades my undershorts?" No way am I doing that.

Besides, the boardwalk is empty. There's nobody for me to scream to.

So I just lie there, sprawled out on the sand. Nothing I can do about it.

The night air is cold. In fact, it's so cold out here, I can't even think of an "it's so cold" joke. My brain is frozen.

And I think I might have broken a bone in my butt. If that's possible.

To be perfectly honest with you, I'm scared.

THANK GOODNESS MY DAD
HAD A BROTHER

Maybe twenty minutes later, I hear this ridiculous singing.

"Shoo-doop 'n' shooby-doo, shoo-doop 'n' shooby-doo…"

It's the opening doo-wop refrain from a tune called "In the Still of the Night," as done by the Five Satins (B-14 on Uncle Frankie's golden-oldies-only jukebox at the diner).

"In the still of the night…" The off-key voice comes closer. *"I-I-I held you, held you ti-i-i-ight."*

I crane my neck and look over at the boardwalk.

It's Uncle Frankie! He's strolling along, flinging out his yo-yo, making kind of sweet Motown moves.

He's basically putting on a private doo-wop
show for the seagulls.

Then he stops, spreads out his arms, and adds
in the harmony: *In the still of the ni-i-i-ight!*

"Uncle Frankie?" I kind of croak the words at
first.

He seems to perk up his ears. Then he definitely looks my way.

"Down here," I cry out.

"Jamie?"

"Yeah."

In a flash, he hops over the railing and comes running toward me, his feet sliding sideways in the sand.

"Are you okay? What happened to you?"

"I dunno. I may have broken a bone in my butt."

He scoops me up. Uncle Frankie is surprisingly strong. I guess it's all that yo-yoing. It must pump up his arm muscles.

"What happened?" he asks again, when I'm safe in his arms.

"Um, I ran into a little trouble."

"Where's your chair?"

"I don't know. I kind of lost it."

He looks me in the eye. I swallow back a tear.

"Okay," he says. "We'll worry about that later, kiddo. Come on. Let's get you home."

And then he carries me off the beach and back up to the boardwalk.

And you know what? I feel just like I used to
    when I was a little kid and fell asleep in the
car. My dad would always pick me up and carry
me into the house.

    I feel safe. I know Uncle Frankie will hold on
tight.

    Just like he said in that song he was singing.

Chapter 25

HOME AGAIN, HOME AGAIN, JIGGITY-JIG...

After a half-mile hike, we make it to Smileyville.

"There you are!" says Aunt Smiley as she comes running out the front door, followed by Uncle Smiley, Ol' Smiler, and Stevie's little brother and sister.

Stevie himself is the last one out the door.

"We were so worried!" says Aunt Smiley. "I called the diner. You must have already closed up."

"Thanks, Frank," says Uncle Smiley.

Uncle Frankie just nods.

"Are you hurt?" my aunt asks. Surprisingly, there is a good deal of kindness in her voice.

"I'm okay," I say. "Just a few bruises."

"And there are no broken bones in his butt," adds Uncle Frankie, who's still holding me in his arms.

The Smileys stare at Uncle Frankie.

He shrugs. "What can I say? We were worried about the boy's butt."

"Somebody dumped this in the alley out back," says Stevie, pushing my wheelchair across the lawn.

Uncle Frankie eases me down into the seat.

The Smileys motion for him to move closer to the stoop so the grown-ups can have a word in private. I hear Aunt Smiley say, "What the heck happened, Frank?" before I feel hot breath in my left ear.

Stevie.

"You tell anybody anything, you're dead meat," he whispers.

I nod.

"And I'll torture you *before* I kill you!"

I nod again.

He jerks my chair forward and pushes me down the driveway like, all of a sudden, he's an orderly and I'm an invalid.

"Let go," I say. "I can do this myself."

"Fine." He lets go by giving me one last shove.

"Jamie?" It's Aunt Smiley. Her whole face is a huge frown. She and Uncle Smiley and Uncle Frankie come over to talk to me. "We were so worried when you didn't come home. We even called the police. Now, what happened?"

I glance over at Stevie.

"I had an accident," I say. "Trust me, accidents happen."

NEW YORK, NEW YORK (SO NICE, THEY NAMED IT TWICE)

On Saturday morning, I hop on the Long Island Rail Road for the hour-long train ride to Penn Station in New York City. I'm making the trip all by myself, and the clueless Smileys don't even notice. Even Stevie Kosgrov isn't tagging along to torment me.

This is sort of a pilgrimage for me. I am journeying to what some people call the comedy capital of the world, the city and comedy clubs where so many stand-ups have gotten their starts.

They call New York "the city that never sleeps" and, judging from some of the characters I'm stuck behind on the sidewalks, it hardly bathes, either.

This whole trip might become a new bit. Me, the country kid from Cornwall, rolling around America's biggest urban jungle. If I'm a fish out of water in Long Beach, I'm a minnow in Manhattan.

I see a blind guy on the corner of Thirty-Ninth Street. He's selling pencils and collecting spare change in a tin cup. When I stop to wait for the light to change, he yells, "Hey, wheelchair kid, you can't beg here. This is my corner. I saw it first."

"I thought you were blind," I say.

"I'm on my ten-minute break. Beat it."

So I roll north, through the mobs of people pushing and shoving. Yes, in New York City it is possible to get run over by a pedestrian. Everybody is eager to tell me where to go, and it isn't exactly Times Square.

Man, I love the city.

Why?

Because in New York City, no one treats me any differently than they treat everybody else.

New Yorkers look at me and my wheelchair the same way they look at the guy with the wild eyes and tattered clothes who knows the world is coming to an end next Tuesday because the leprechaun in his pocket just told him so.

They completely ignore us.

Yep—there's very little pity on the streets of the big city. I♥NY!

Chapter 27

WELCOME TO THE COMEDY CAPITAL OF THE WORLD!

I can't believe I'm sitting on Broadway outside Carolines, one of the most famous comedy clubs in the country. Everybody's appeared here: Jay Leno, Jerry Seinfeld, Colin Quinn, Elayne Boosler, Louis C.K., Chris Rush. The list goes on and on.

I see a poster for that Planet's Funniest Kid Comic Contest in the "Coming Attractions" display case.

I guess Carolines is hosting the local contest for New York City, like the Comedy Club in Ronkonkoma is hosting the preliminary round out on Long Island. Yes. I checked out the Planet's Funniest Kid Comic website after Uncle Frankie told me about the competition.

That doesn't mean that I'm entering it. Far from it. Just that I know how to surf the Web without wiping out. I'm still confident I'd gag if I ever got onstage in front of an audience.

I roll into a nearby souvenir shop because I want to get Uncle Frankie an I♥NY yo-yo. No luck. I♥NY is on everything from thimbles to pens to boxer shorts, but no yo-yos. Someone needs to write the mayor. "Yo! We need some yo-yos."

So I grab a snow globe. Which gives me another idea for a bit: You ever wonder what it would be like to be a tiny person living inside a snow-globe city? The TV weather reports would be interesting: "Chance of an upside-down earthquake followed by a ten-second blizzard and a tsunami."

I pick up a foam rubber Statue of Liberty crown for myself. I'm thinking I might use it in my act. I could pretend I'm going to take over for her. "Poor lady, she's been standing in the harbor since 1886, holding up that torch. Her arm has got to be tired. This is why the woman never smiles. And that gown...whose idea was that? There's no shade, and she's standing out there in the hot sun in a toga made out of sheet metal?"

Yeah. New York is treating me the way it's always treated comedians. It's giving me a ton of material!

Too bad nobody except the folks at Uncle Frankie's diner will ever get to hear any of it.

Chapter 28

RUDE AND CRUDE,
WITH MY KIND OF 'TUDE

My next stop is the Ed Sullivan Theater, up on Broadway and Fifty-Fourth Street, where David Letterman tapes his show.

I'm kind of in total awe, just thinking about all the great comics who have appeared on this stage. Some of them probably even used *this very same sidewalk* to get to that stage.

You know, people will tell you that New Yorkers are so rude they don't even get along with each other. But Letterman says that's not true: "I saw two New Yorkers, complete strangers, sharing a cab. One guy took the tires and the radio; the other guy took the engine."

In New York, they say people go to hockey games for the fighting. In the stands. To participate.

So during my entire visit, not one single New Yorker acts extra nice to me because I'm in a wheelchair.

And I love every minute of it!

Check it out:

A taxi splashes me because I stop too close to the gutter.

A tour bus nearly runs me down in a crosswalk because I don't realize that the traffic signals in the city are just "suggestions."

I learn you should never, ever travel *behind* a horse-drawn carriage in Central Park.

While I'm waiting for the subway to head back to Penn Station, a rat the size of an otter scampers up from the tracks just so it can pee on my shoe.

This whole city is hilarious.

Including the subway ride to Penn Station. A guy mugs me, armed only with a finger pistol under his hoodie. I give him my last two bucks. He hops off at the next stop. I just smile and wave as he runs away.

"Go with God," I say.

Because he robbed me just like he'd rob anybody else!

Chapter 29

A NEW WEEK, A NEW ME (EVEN THOUGH I LOOK A LOT LIKE THE OLD ME!)

Refreshed from my weekend trip to the city, I start the new week at school with a renewed sense of purpose. I promise myself I will persistently pursue perfecting the three Ps! (Try saying *that* three times fast in front of a mirror without splattering it with spit!)

I will also follow Uncle Frankie's advice and try to finally figure out how to stop choking.

I will *practice* my act (in the privacy of my bedroom).

I will *prepare* new material (thanks again, NYC).

I will *perform*. In front of people. (Maybe.)

That last P is the hardest one. Where am I supposed to try out my material before I take it to the comedy club in Ronkonkoma?

If I decide to enter. That's a huge IF. About twice the size of one of those billboards in Times Square. Instead of a giant Abercrombie & Fitch "A" and "F," picture a humongous "I-F."

But *if* I maybe, possibly (weather permitting) do enter, I need to perform somewhere else first.

Suddenly, the obvious answer hits me: Why not at school?

Talk about your captive audience. These people are glued to their seats for fifty minutes at a time. I could become the class clown. And since my pals Gilda, Gaynor, and Pierce are in my math class, I decide to make math my first show of the day.

Okay, here goes nothing—or should I say *everything*?

I raise my hand.

"Yes, Mr. Grimm?" says the teacher, Ms. Zick. "Do you have a question?"

"No. I'm just auditioning to be the new Statue of Liberty."

"Excuse me?"

"Have you seen the statue lately? She's not looking good. In fact, she looks kind of green."

People (the teacher not included) start chuckling.

"I think it's because she's been holding up her arm for over a century. Her fingers have got to be tingling. And what about that BO?" I fan my free hand under my armpit for emphasis. "Whoo! Somebody sign this poor lady up for a new deodorant."

Everybody is laughing like crazy—except, of course, Ms. Zick. She's basically scowling.

"Mr. Grimm?" she says, extremely grimly.

But I can't stop. I'm *performing*! My audience is laughing.

"That smell in Bayonne? It isn't New Jersey. It's *her*."

Pierce, Gaynor, and Gilda actually applaud.

The teacher does not. She goes to her desk, finds the dreaded pink pad, and writes me up.

Yep. I just earned my first detention *ever*.

I know I should feel ashamed, but actually I'm kind of proud of myself.

Pierce, Gaynor, and Gilda? They're *definitely* proud of me.

When school ends, I head with my fellow felons to detention hall.

Stevie Kosgrov is already in the room. I think he's a detention regular. Rumor has it that the principal herself gave Kosgrov a life sentence without parole. Stevie's two thuggish friends from that night on the boardwalk (when I learned I could fly, if properly flung) are in detention, too. Zits and Useless, if I remember right, which I do. I'm wondering if we're all going to make license plates, like they do in prison movies.

"Congratulations," says Stevie. "You made it to the Big House. Maybe you're not a total weenie."

I guess I should feel proud that I was funny enough to cause a disturbance. But I don't. I feel terrible. Like when you let your parents down. Or get caught cheating at Monopoly. Or both.

There's not much for me to do in detention hall except watch time tick by. Have you ever noticed that school clocks are the slowest clocks in the world? It's like the principal has a secret space-time continuum warper hidden in her office

124

that turns school days into dog years.

"Mr. Grimm?" says Mrs. Kanai. She's a nice lady. Good teacher, too. Guess she drew the short straw in the faculty lounge today and got detention duty. "Can I see you at my desk?" She gestures for me to come to the front of the room.

All the hard-core convicts in the room have their beady eyes trained on me as I roll up the aisle.

"Yes, ma'am?" I whisper.

"What are you doing in detention, Jamie?" she whispers back.

I shrug my shoulders. "I cracked a couple of jokes in math class."

"Well, how will you get home?"

"The usual way, I guess."

"Is there a special bus you take?"

"No. I live pretty close by."

"Still, it must take you a long time to…" She catches herself. I can tell she wanted to say "walk home." So I help her out.

"It's not so bad. I do it every day."

"Well, I don't like the idea of you out there on the street this late. It's getting dark earlier and earlier. I think you've learned your lesson."

I look down at my lap because I can tell that Mrs. Kanai is feeling sorry for me. She can't help herself. Like I said, she's nice.

But I hate when that happens.

I earned my detention the old-fashioned way. I shouldn't be given a "Get Out of Jail Free" card just because I'm in this chair.

"I'm going to let you go early," says Mrs. Kanai.

I check out the clock. I have served exactly twelve minutes of my one-hour sentence.

I take a quick glance at my fellow detainees. From the looks on their faces, they hate me as much as I hate being given any kind of special treatment.

"Can Steve Kosgrov be excused early, too?" I ask.

"Kosgrov?" Mrs. Kanai checks her warden sheet. Stevie is scheduled for detention from now until some time after he finishes junior college.

"He's my"—I fight my gag reflex—"adoptive brother."

"Oh, will he help you get home safely?"

I go ahead and fib. Actually, this is definitely a lie. "Yes, ma'am."

"Well, I think that will be okay. Just this one time."

And Stevie gets sprung, too.

SAYING THANKS
UNTIL IT HURTS

To say thanks for his early release, Stevie punches me in the shoulder.

To add a *muchas gracias*, he wallops me in the other shoulder.

At least I'll have matching bruises. Purple, I hope. It's one of my favorite colors.

"You're welcome," I say when Stevie is finished expressing his gratitude with his fists.

"Don't get cocky, Cornball. This earns you nothing. Besides, you left my two beach buddies behind."

"I'm sorry. I don't know their actual names. Besides, none of that stuff on the boardwalk with my wheelchair ever happened. Remember?"

"Shuddup. I'll see you at home. And, you'll see *me* in your nightmares!"

The guy is totally gloating.

I nod and give him a weak little wave.

"Right," I say. "Looking forward to it. Can't wait. Counting the seconds."

Can you imagine living in the same house with that guy? Even in the adjoining garage?

No. You. Can't.

Chapter 32

MY MYSTERY GIRL

While I'm sitting there in the hall, an extremely cool-looking girl comes strolling by—and then she stops right in front of me. *What's this all about?*

She's holding a stack of books.

And that's about all she's doing, besides grinning and silently checking me out. *Very* silently. It's so quiet in the hall, I can hear crickets—and we're nowhere near the science lab.

I'm also *extremely* nervous. As nervous as a weatherman with a bad comb-over who's doing typhoon coverage.

I've accidentally added a fourth P to "practice, prepare, and perform"—*perspire*.

Finally, since I've had so much practice at it, I say my name. "Um, hi. I'm Jamie Grimm."

"I know who you are," says the cool girl.

And then it's crickets time again. Only now I can hear a drop of my flop sweat plinking to the floor, too.

"So, that's a lot of books," I say because I can't think of anything else to say. "Can I help you carry them?"

"Sure. Why not?"

She plops her books in my lap, turns, and walks away.

One of them is a physics book, and I suddenly realize this is the girl I've been accused of gawking at.

"Just leave them at locker 219," she says over her shoulder.

Okay. That's pretty cool. Dumping her books in my lap. Sashaying away. Not a care in the world.

Suddenly, she stops and pivots on her heel, like she's this supercool supermodel.

Then she ambles back toward me, slow and easy. In my head, I'm hearing a jazz saxophone solo. And not the kind the guy in the school's marching band honks out. A good one. Like Lisa Simpson would play.

Because this girl, as I've said, is extremely cool. I wouldn't be surprised if she wears sunglasses when she goes to sleep.

"I know your name," she says, "because I voted for you, Jamie Grimm."

"F-f-for student council?" I stammer.

"Yes. Were you running for something else?"

"No. Not that I know of."

Okay. Mystery solved. This cool girl is the third person who voted for me.

New mystery: *Why did she vote for me?*

"Not that you asked," she says, "but my name is Suzie Orolvsky."

"Cool," I say. I don't mention anything about how it won't fit on my knuckles.

And even though I know her real name, I don't think I'll be calling her Suzie too often.

For me, she will always be Cool Girl.

Chapter 33

CLOUDY WITH A CHANCE OF BRAINSTORMS

Inspired by the small confidence boost during my post-detention moment with Cool Girl, I have a brainstorm.

And, not to brag, but it's kind of almost genius!

I know how to nail that final *perform* P—where to try out my act to see if I'm worthy of the Planet's Funniest Kid Comic Contest.

EUREKA!

This will be a true torture test. But: I have to make the Smileys laugh!

Wish me luck. Concrete statues in bird fountains chuckle more often than these people.

Chapter 34

HOME IS WHERE THE LAUGHS AREN'T

I give it my best shot.

At the dinner table, I tell food jokes.

"What do you call cheese that isn't your own?"

They just stare. So I hit them with the punch line: "Nacho cheese."

Nothing. Not even a baby nose snort.

I try again when they're all watching television.

"So, did you hear about the guy who spent all day watching football and fell asleep in front of the television? The next morning, his wife wakes him up. 'Get up, honey,' she says. 'It's twenty to seven.' 'Really?' says the guy. 'Who's winning?'"

Again, I get nothing. Not even a whimper from the dog.

So I try some bathroom humor.

"Why did Piglet, Eeyore, and Christopher Robin stick their heads down the toilet? Easy. They were looking for Pooh."

Nada. Zip. Zero.

But I don't give up.

Later, I try out a middle-of-the-night joke.

"Hey, did you hear about the dummy who sat up all night wondering where the sun had gone? The next morning, it dawned on him."

They don't laugh. They tell me to go to bed.

I try one more time. I give Ol' Smiler a command performance.

"So, did you hear about the dog who went to the flea circus? He stole the whole show. Say, why do dogs wag their tails? Because no one else will do it for them."

I finally get a response.

It's a growl.

I give up. Forget the Planet's Funniest Kid Comic Contest.

I wasn't even the funniest kid in the backyard.

Chapter 35

FINALLY, A GOOD DREAM

But that same night, I have a dream.

And it's not my usual nightmare about Stevie punching me in the nose until my head explodes like the balloon over the clown's face in the water-gun arcade.

This is a *good* dream. I'm talking with one of my idols, comedy legend Billy Crystal.

"I grew up on Long Island, too," he says.

"I know."

"In high school, I was the class comedian as opposed to the class clown. The difference is, the class clown is the guy who drops his pants at the football game; the class comedian is the guy who talked him into it."

"I tried being the class clown."

"I know. I saw. That bit with the Statue of Liberty crown. You don't have to try so hard to be funny because, trust me, Jamie, you *are* funny."

"I funny."

"What? Are we doing foreign dialects now?"

"It's something a customer, Mr. Burdzecki, said to me at the diner. He's Russian. He said, 'You funny.'"

"*Da*," says Billy. "I agree. You funny. I sleepy. Go knock 'em dead up in Ronkonkoma, kid. Just let *you* be *you*. Let people see how you see the world."

I wake up. It's the middle of the night. Eureka! I know what I must do.

That dream was a sign.

I am definitely going to enter the contest in Ronkonkoma and take my shot at being crowned Long Island's Funniest Kid Comic!

Yes, it's the stupidest thing anybody has ever done.

Yes, I'll probably be crushed and humiliated and suffer greatly.

Yes, I will probably ruin my best shirt with permanent sweat stains.

But I'm going to do it anyway because, to mangle a line from one of Billy Crystal's movies, when you realize you want to spend the rest of your life doing something, you want the rest of your life to start as soon as possible.

Of course, I won't tell anybody my plans. I'm too embarrassed. Too scared. What if they want to come watch me? What if I'm terrible?

I won't even tell Uncle Frankie. And I feel super guilty about it. He's always been my biggest fan. Heck, he's the one who told me about the comedy contest in the first place. But I just can't have him there. What if it turns out I *not* funny? I don't want to break his heart. If I lose, I'll stick with just breaking my own.

I check the website one last time. The Long Island contest is Saturday, less than a week away. How can I possibly get myself ready by then? What if I choke? What if I get the yips?

When I leave the house the next morning, I am a man on a mission: I am determined that before this week is over, I will be named Long Island's Funniest Kid Comic!

HOW DO YOU GET TO RONKONKOMA? PRACTICE, PRACTICE, PRACTICE

I spend the rest of the week worrying about the upcoming competition.

Do I have enough material? Is it funny enough? Am *I* funny enough?

I work up a whole bit about a small town called Grossville and try it out on Gaynor and Pierce:

"The other day, the kid sitting behind me in class sneezed all over the back of my head. 'Don't worry,' he said. 'I'm not contagious. It's just allergies.' Actually, I was more worried about the boogers in my hair than my health. Then I found out this kid, he lives in Grossville. You guys ever been there?"

Gaynor and Pierce play along. They shake
their heads and yell, "NO!" like they're my rowdy
audience in a comedy club.

"Oh, let me tell you, in Grossville they sneeze
on each other all the time. It's why everybody's
hair is so green. Yeah, you think it's funny, but
it's snot. When kids in Grossville say, 'Mommy,
can I lick the bowl?' their mothers say, 'Be quiet,
dear, and just flush.'"

My test audience is cracking up.

But I don't stop. All over Long Beach, I'm
trying out lines—on myself, total strangers, even
a few seagulls I bribe with bread crumbs.

I really want to do a bit about political correctness. That means using soft and fuzzy words to make sure you never say anything that'll hurt anybody's feelings by telling them the cold, hard truth. For instance, instead of calling the food in the cafeteria "crap," you could call it "digestively challenging." And I'm not crippled or handicapped; I'm "differently abled."

I even riff with this guy Squeegee, who hangs out near a Dumpster behind the bait shop.

"My school is so politically correct, nobody's fat anymore. Everyone is just 'horizontally expanded.'"

"That's really funny, kid," he says. "You're a stitch. Spare a dollar for a cup of coffee?"

Chapter 37

SNEAKING OUT OF TOWN

The big day is finally here!

I want to get an early start. Ronkonkoma is forty miles east of Long Beach, so I've got a bit of a trip ahead of me.

The Crack of Dawn

And I don't want any of the Smileys (especially Stevie) to know where I'm going. Yes, I'm taking full advantage of my garage door bedroom. I'm sneaking out of the house.

Since the Planet's Funniest Kid Comic Contest is a special event at the comedy club, showtime is slated for pretty early (for a *night*club): 2 PM.

I hope I live that long.

I'm a nervous wreck. My toes are trembling. My teeth are chattering. My heart is pounding so loudly, it's like somebody's jackhammering inside my rib cage.

I wonder if I'll be the first kid to die of a heart attack.

What if they have to give me CPR while I'm onstage? If they do, I hope I at least make funny squeak-toy noises when they thump on my chest.

It's way early, but I see this scraggly guy walking up the street holding a sign announcing the end of the world.

Yeah, right. Everybody's a comedian.

I check my bags one last time to make sure I have all my props and junk.

The cab I called is waiting for me at the corner. But the driver almost pulls away when he sees my wheelchair.

"Don't worry!" I shout. "You can just toss a lot of this crap in the trunk."

"Fine. That takes care of you and the bags. But what am I gonna do with the freakin' wheelchair?"

Yep. *Everybody's* a comedian.

YIKES! IT'S SHOWTIME!

Finally, I'm onstage.

The place is packed. I guess the twelve other contestants invited their entire families—from grandparents to third cousins—plus all their friends from school.

And all I can think is, "Where'd that guy say the nearest fire exit is?"

I want to bolt because I am freaked out beyond belief. If there's something worse than choking (backward barfing, perhaps?), I'm doing it.

My mind is a total and complete blank.

All I can remember are the punch lines from my jokes, none of the setups.

(Yeah, this is where you came in.)

I close my eyes. Just for a second. I think
about Uncle Frankie, my biggest fan (who,
thankfully, isn't here to see me, live onstage and
dying). I concentrate on the three Ps. I think
about my Billy Crystal dream: "You don't have to
try so hard to be funny because, trust me, Jamie,
you *are* funny." And Mr. Burdzecki: "You funny
boy!"

Right. *I funny.*

I open my eyes. Take a deep breath.

Here goes everything.

"Um, hi," I squeak out. "The other day at school we had this substitute teacher. Very tough. Sort of like Mrs. Darth Vader. Had the heavy breathing, the deep voice. During roll call, she said, 'Are you chewing gum, young man?' And I said, 'No, I'm Jamie Grimm.'"

Yes! I remembered the punch line and the setup. And the audience is actually chuckling.

Okay. Time to address the eight-hundred-pound gorilla in the room. Not the club's bouncer. My wheelchair.

I hit them with my second joke.

"Wow, what a crowd," I say, surveying the packed audience. "Standing room only. Good thing I brought my own chair."

It takes a second, but they laugh—right after I let them know it's okay to laugh because *I'm* smiling. The laugh builds. I even get a smattering of applause. On my *second* joke! That could be some kind of new indoor record.

I just hope the applause lasts. For, like, ten more minutes.

Because, sorry—I'm choking again. I can't remember the setup to joke number three. Or four, five, six—any of them. Now I'm hoping I *do* have a heart attack so I'll be dead before I totally bomb.

The three judges are sitting at the table closest to the stage.

One of them, a very sweet woman with funky red glasses, leans forward a little and whispers, "Don't worry, Jamie. You're already a winner in my book. It took a lot of courage for you to get up on that stage."

There, there. Don't cry! You deserve a medal because you're still breathing.

Okay. I'm sure Ms. Redglasses Nicelady means well. But she's judging me by my wheelchair, not by who I am or what I might have to say.

She's treating me special.

And, as you know, *I hate when that happens*!

This comedy competition is in danger of turning into a pity party.

And so I let 'em have it. With both barrels.

TAKING NO PRISONERS

*S*uddenly, I remember every punch line and every setup from every joke I ever read or wrote!

"So," I say, "can you believe it? I got a ticket for parking out front in the handicapped parking space."

The audience groans in sympathy.

"Yeah. I know. It was horrible. Of course, the ticket wasn't so much for *where* I parked. I think it had more to do with the whole 'underage driving' thing. Yeah, according to the cop, I have to be old enough for a driver's license before I can park anywhere.

"So, I live down in Long Beach, also known as the land of the living dead. Every morning there are all these zombies roaming the streets. Well, I call them zombies. You probably call them 'commuters.' This one zombie has a new girlfriend. He introduced her to his buddy, and the guy said, 'Wow, she's a hottie. Where'd you dig her up?'

"Anyway, it's good to be here for the Planet's Funniest Kid Comic Contest. It was either this or *Dancing with the Stars*. I can tango, but my fox-trot stinks."

They laugh louder. I'm actually *on a roll*.

I take them on a funny tour of United Nations Beach. I do a quick bit about living in a snow-globe city and trying to buy flood insurance. We discuss the Statue of Liberty's body-odor issues. We head down to Grossville for a few booger jokes.

And then I launch into my closer. My anti–political correctness piece.

"At my school everybody works hard at being PC. You know, 'politically correct.' They try to soften their words so they never blurt out the cold, hard truth. Nobody farts anymore. We just 'expel alternative fuels.' Kids in kindergarten don't listen to 'Jack and the Beanstalk,' either. It's now 'Jack and the Dangers of Genetically Engineered Bean Seeds.'"

I look right at my sympathetic judge (who, BTW, is laughing so hard, the tears in her eyes have fogged up her glasses).

"And, as you know, I'm not handicapped, I'm 'differently abled.' That's why I feel sorry for you guys. You're all so 'ordinarily abled.' Bor-ring."

I toss in a quick Church Lady voice from *Saturday Night Live* reruns.

"'*Now isn't that special?*' You 'ordinary' people still have to use your legs to get around. Me? I just sit on my butt. I can be a couch potato twenty-four/seven—at home *and* on the go. You guys have to stand up when you ride an elevator. When the sidewalk slants downhill, you don't get to coast. You have to feel guilty if you use the handicap stall when the tiny one right next to it is empty. Not me.

"You know, with all my different abilities, I'm sort of like Superman or Spider-Man—I just don't have to wear a mask or funny tights. 'Now isn't *that* special?'"

They're really cheering now. Some people are even standing up to applaud. It's time to get offstage. I throw them all a huge wave.

"Thank you! I'm Jamie Grimm. And you folks have been very, very *special*."

Chapter 40

TIME CRAWLS WHEN YOU'RE DONE HAVING FUN

And then we wait—all the contestants.
Together.

Thirteen kid comics take the stage, do five or ten minutes of jokes, and then retreat to the back of the club, where we get to watch everybody do way better than we thought we did ourselves.

It's sort of like the Red Room on *American Idol*, only without all the free Coca-Cola.

We wait for days.

Months.

Decades.

I may need to learn how to shave.

How did I do? I don't know. It was such a rush being onstage, riding the waves of laughter. But

I have no idea if I was good enough. Plus, there's nobody here to pat me on the back and say, "Awesome! Way to go!"

I know. That's my fault. I didn't tell anybody how I planned on spending my Saturday this weekend. Now I sort of wish that I had.

The kids who are my competition? Like I said, they're a tight-lipped bunch when they aren't telling jokes onstage. They're all in it to win it. They almost make the Smileys seem warm and fuzzy.

Finally, the last kid comic takes her bows.

The three judges huddle together at their table.

One of them, an adult comic who's a regular at the club, walks onstage and grabs the microphone.

"Ladies and gentlemen, the judges have voted. We're ready to announce the winner of the Long Island's Funniest Kid Comic competition."

He takes a *huge* pause.

"Right after the break."

Great. It *is* just like *American Idol*.

MAY I HAVE THE ENVELOPE, PLEASE?

Finally, after what feels like another decade, the countdown begins.

"The third runner-up is…Ronna Applebaum!"

I'd like to thank everybody I've ever met in my whole life! My kindergarten teacher, the hall monitor…

Her family screams. I think she wins a T-shirt and some free jalapeño poppers.

"The second runner-up is...Michael Miller!"

More applause. Michael Miller races up to the stage to grab his trophy and gift certificates.

"The first runner-up..."

Okay—isn't the first runner-up just *the runner-up*? Yes, my mind is wandering because I'm positive I don't have a chance of winning anything, not even a souvenir baseball cap or some  free French fries. Hey, I heard the routines of the third and second runners-up. They were both hysterical.

"...Billy Hester!"

Now I'm wondering if I went too far. Maybe I should've skipped the anti-PC bit and stuck to my booger jokes.

"And the winner of Long Island's Funniest

Kid Comic competition, the young comic who moves on to the New York State competition… can I get a drum roll…is…the one and only…the irrepressible…the person whose name I'm about to read…because it's written on this card…JAMIE GRIMM!"

Now I might really have that heart attack.

This is totally un-freakin'-believable. My competitors? They're all smiling and clapping and cheering for me as I roll up to the stage. "Way to go, Grimm!" "You killed big!" "Awesome set, Jamie!"

I'm so happy I could *run* all the way home. Seriously!

Unfortunately, I have to haul my wheelchair back to Smileyville. And there are no taxis. Guess I'll have to schlep back to Long Beach on the bus. Fortunately, there *is* a bus.

Still, a win is a win!
I just wish...

Well, I wish my mom and dad could've seen me win.

That's all. I just wish they both could've been here.

Funny how life works out sometimes, huh?

Yeah. Really, really funny.

PART TWO
The Long, Winding, Twisting, Curving, Sloping, Slippery-When-Wet Road Home

HERO FOR A DAY!

So I'm guessing that one of the other kids from Long Island's Funniest Kid Comic Contest tweets on Twitter.

I also think one of the runners-up must have at least six billion Facebook friends.

And I'll bet somebody in the audience blogs, too.

Because word about what happened at the comedy club in Ronkonkoma on Saturday is all over Long Beach Middle School first thing Monday morning.

Suddenly, I'm the hometown hero! Me. In Long Beach. For the first time since forever, I'm a winner, not a loser.

Kids (including ninth graders) carry me into school on their shoulders like I'm a pharaoh or something.

The marching band puts on a parade, complete with a formation that spells out my name and includes a tuba player running over to dot the *i* in *Jamie*. The cafeteria ladies bake me a sheet cake so huge that the janitor has to haul it around on a forklift—*after* they use a heavy-duty crane to hoist it out of the kitchen. The cheerleaders give me my own personal pep rally.

It is an unbelievably amazing way to start the day.

Okay. You're right, you're right. You're always right. None of that happened.

But a bunch of people in the halls did knock knuckles with me and slap me high fives and say stuff like "Yo, way to go" and "Awesome, dude." Which was major.

In fact, it felt even better than a pharaoh parade with cheerleaders and free cake.

Chapter 43

OKAY, HALF A DAY

By lunchtime that brief but fantastic triumphant feeling is completely and totally gone. Because by now *other* people had started tweeting, texting, and blogging. Snarky people who have some pretty strong—okay, nasty— opinions about why I won on Saturday.

"The judges felt sorry for you?" Pierce reports when he checks his phone in the cafeteria.

"Somebody sent me a text," reports Gilda. "According to this, you won on pity points."

"What?"

"Yeah," says Gaynor, reading the screen on his phone. "This blogger, some dude named A. Nonny Mouse, says, 'The judges felt sorry for Jamie Grimm, a contestant as lame as the jokes he was telling. He didn't win. His wheelchair did.'"

All of a sudden, I feel like someone just socked me in the gut with a shovel. I can barely breathe. I want to hide under the table and never come out again.

"Here's another blog," says Gilda with a defeated sigh. "'Jamie Grimm wasn't funny. He was sad and pathetic. No wonder his name is grim, as in dismal and depressing.'"

"Well," I say, trying to joke through the pain, "at least that one is educational. He taught his readers a new vocabulary word."

"It sucks the big radish, Jamie," says Gaynor. I have no idea what the big radish is, either. It's pure Gaynor, though.

"Whoever wrote this junk is just jealous," adds Gilda. "Sore losers, but definitely *losers*."

"Precisely," says Pierce. "They can't diminish your accomplishment by trashing it."

See? I told you these guys were great friends. Gilda, too.

Unfortunately, there are only three of them.

Word has quickly spread about the "real" reason for my victory, and now the whole cafeteria is laughing at me. Yes, comedians live for laughter, but not this kind. These are more like mean snickers, plus finger-pointing and loud whispers. They're not laughing because of some joke I just told. They're laughing because they think *I'm* the joke.

I need to get out of the cafeteria and hide somewhere nice and quiet.

So I head for the library. Where else would you hide in school?

I see Stevie Kosgrov finger-typing like a maniac on a computer with one hand while thumbing the keypad of his smartphone with the other. He's so busy clacking keys, he doesn't hear me when I roll up right behind him and look over his shoulder to see what he's writing:

JAMIE GRIMM ONLY WON BECAUSE THE SAPPY JUDGES FELT SORRY FOR HIM.

Stevie hits the Send button and finally figures out I'm sitting right behind him.

When he whips around, he's smiling like somebody just crowned *him* Long Island's comedy king.

Chapter 44

COOL GIRL TO THE RESCUE

Suzie Orolvsky (aka Cool Girl) is also in the library.

After Stevie leaves, she comes over and plops her books in my lap.

The girl studies a lot of heavy subjects, all with textbooks the size of cinder blocks. Plus, she reads whatever she's in the mood for, and she's got a lot of different moods. Today it's *Inheritance*, another thick book.

"Let's walk," she says.

"Actually," I say, "my doctors tell me that would take a medical miracle."

Cool Girl doesn't laugh. She rotates her wrist and presses a button on her sports watch.

"See this?" she says. "It's a stopwatch. New rules:

For the next five minutes, you cannot crack a joke or attempt, in any way, to be funny."

"Don't worry. Haven't you heard? I not funny. I pathetic."

"You mean those stupid blogs and text messages?"

"Yeah. Them."

"The way I see it, Jamie, the blogs love you, the blogs hate you. You ever notice that *blogger* is only two letters away from *booger*?"

"Hey, you said no jokes."

"For *you*. Plus, that wasn't much of a joke." She head gestures toward the exit. "Come on."

We roll and stroll along the hallway.

"You know, Jamie, the way you use comedy is a lot like being politically correct."

"What?" Now I'm a little confused.

"You use jokes to hide your true feelings the way other people soften their words so they never blurt out the cold, hard truth."

"Wait a second...."

"Yeah. I stole that last line from you. I caught your act on YouTube."

"It's on YouTube?"

She nods. "Not the best camera work. A little shaky. You see a lot of this one doofus's head. But somebody did, indeed, record you and your act on a cell phone. And you know what?"

"What?"

"You were great. Seriously hysterical."

"Really?"

"Yep. I heard all those people in the club yukking it up, too. Then, at the end, they gave you a standing ovation."

"Well, I couldn't give one to myself."

"Jamie? Your five minutes aren't up."

"Sorry."

"They didn't give you that trophy because they felt sorry for you. They gave it to you because *you're funny*!"

"Thanks."

"You're also funny-looking."

"What?"

"Lighten up. It's a joke."

"So when do I get to put *you* in the five-minute penalty box?"

She smiles. It's a wickedly good smile, too. She's not called Cool Girl for nothing.

"We'll talk," she says. "Oh—that bit about chicken nuggets? I used it today in the cafeteria. Cracked everybody up. We're talking milk-out-the-nostrils laughter. So I have only one question: How come you didn't ask me to go with you to the big contest?"

"Well, I...I...well, I didn't know you cared."

"Who says I care?"

She sashays away, leaving me holding her books. Again.

Girls. Who can understand them? Not me. I'm just the local bookmobile.

NOTE TO SELF:
TELL UNCLE FRANKIE!

After school I head off to Uncle Frankie's diner, where nobody knows that I'm a huge celebrity.

I help out behind the cash register, making change and making jokes.

My George Carlin fan comes to the counter with a newspaper tucked under his arm.

I ring him up and give him a choice Carlin one-liner: "Isn't it kind of scary that doctors call what they do 'practice'?"

He cracks up and puts down his newspaper to dig in his pockets for cash to cover his check.

That's when I see the headline over a small article on page thirty-eight, back near the ads for free kittens: LONG BEACH LOCAL JAMIE GRIMM WINS COMEDY CONTEST.

Now I have to tell Uncle Frankie *before* he hears about it from somebody else or, worse, reads about it when he's cleaning up the newspapers people leave behind in the booths.

I roll into the kitchen, where Uncle Frankie is yo-yoing with one hand while plunging a basket of fries into the deep fryer with the other. Fortunately, he never gets confused. If he did, we'd be serving our customers deep-fried plastic, and he'd be Walking the Dog with shoestring potatoes.

"Um, Uncle Frankie?"

"Hey, Jamie. What's up? Howyadoinkid?"

"I need to tell you something."

"Hey, you can tell me anything. I mean that. Always remember that, kiddo, okay?"

"Okay."

"So—is this about some girl?"

"No. Not really. It's about last Saturday."

He looks a little confused. "Last Saturday? Were we supposed to go fishing?"

"No. Not fishing."

"Good, 'cause it's too cold to go fishing." He's reeling his yo-yo up and down, up and down. It helps Uncle Frankie think, or so he tells me.

"It's about that comedy contest you told me about."

"Oh, yeah. When is that?"

"Last Saturday."

"And we missed it?"

"No. I mean *you* did, but I didn't."

"You went?"

"Yeah."

"You told jokes?"

"Yeah."

"How'd you do?"

"Not bad."

"Good for you, kiddo. Because winning isn't everything. In fact, in our diner softball league, we like to say, 'If you had fun, you won.'"

"I won."

Uncle Frankie smiles. "So you had fun?"

"No..."

Now he frowns. "It wasn't fun?"

"Well, kind of. Yeah. But, I *won* won."

"You *won* won?"

"Yeah. I *won*!"

"You're Long Island's Funniest Kid Comic?"

I shrug. "That's what they say."

"Well, they're right. Because that's what I say, too! Come here, you!"

He rushes over to give me a big bear hug, which feels so good.

"I'm sorry I didn't tell you about it," I say. "I was so nervous. I thought I might bomb and—"

"No need to explain, Jamie. I understand completely. My first yo-yo competition? I didn't tell anybody either. Not my mother, not my father, not my sister, not my little brother..."

"Did you win?"

"Well, let's just say I had fun."

And then he hugs me some more, which feels even better than the first hug.

"Jamie, I am so proud of you. You worked hard. You never gave up. That took guts, kiddo. Courage. And you know what?"

"What?"

"When you do stuff like that, you remind me of *him*."

"My dad?"

Uncle Frankie nods. "Yeah. My brave little brother."

Chapter 46

FEELING THE LOVE...
AND JUST A LITTLE HATE

Back at school the next day, Mrs. Kanai, my ELA teacher, compliments me on my big win.

She's actually gushing a little.

"Congratulations, Jamie! All the teachers are talking about your triumph."

"Thanks."

Warning: If head gets too big, it will EXPLODE!

"I've never had a famous comedian in my class before. So, did you use any of your hilarious 'climbing Mount Everest' speech in your routine?"

"No. Not this time."

"Oh? Is there a next time?"

"Well, I guess I'm supposed to represent Long Island at the New York State competition. Um, actually, I *know* I am."

"And when's that?"

"In a couple of weeks. In Manhattan. A comedy club called Gotham."

"How exciting! Congratulations again, Jamie. I know you'll win the next round, too."

Wow. You have no idea how good it makes me feel to hear Mrs. Kanai say stuff like that...even if it's not true.

And then there are my buds. Gaynor, Pierce, Gilda, and Cool Girl. They're all pulling for me, too. Asking me what bits I'm going to do for the next round. Pumping me up. Telling me I'm going to win again.

Yes, I have a very small and mostly nerdy fan club. And much to my amazement, it grows a little larger every day. Apparently, these new recruits liked what they saw of my act on YouTube (even though *everybody* wishes that doofus blocking the camera had a smaller head).

"That blogger was so wrong," one after another tells me. "I caught your act. You were good, man!"

Even the vice principal—the school's head disciplinarian, the man who collects the detention slips and memorizes every name on them, Mr. Sour Patch himself—actually nods at me in the hallway. Just once. But it is an official nod. Pierce is my witness.

As for Stevie Kosgrov?

He's still giving me the finger. About a thousand times a day.

You gotta love the guy.

Chapter 47

TIME FOR A LITTLE Q&A

Later in the week, on an absolutely awesome afternoon, Cool Girl and I head to the boardwalk.

I'm thinking she needs me to carry her books all the way home for her. But she just wants to sit and talk.

Check out the lovebirds!

About the future. You know: college, kids, an NFL career, the Boston Marathon.

"I'm also thinking about the Roller Derby," I say. "After I have a couple of concussions playing football, of course."

"Of course."

She rocks her wrist and hits the start button on her stopwatch.

Yeah, we do the five-minute funny-free deal every now and then. It's a little like truth or dare, only we don't ask each other stuff like "If you woke up one day and you were invisible, what is the first thing you would do?"

"Okay," she says. "I have to ask you a serious question."

"I know. I heard the stopwatch beep."

"Jamie?"

"I wasn't being funny. I was just stating the facts."

"But with a tone. A funny tone."

"Fine," I say. "No more tone."

"Okay. So." She braces both her hands on her knees. Hesitates. "I'm kind of curious...."

"Okay."

She hesitates some more.

I get the feeling that this is a tough question for her to ask. Which probably means it'll be even tougher for me to answer.

"How do you take a whiz?"

"What?"

"Can you, you know, pee?"

"No," I say sarcastically. "I've been holding it in for two years. That's why I make that sloshing sound. My bladder is one gigantic water balloon. Stand back—I'm about to blow."

Totally embarrassed, I make a hasty retreat.

I mean, it's just too weird. "How do you take a whiz?" "Can you pee?" Who asks questions like that?

But once my face goes from code purple to somewhere closer to my normal skin tone, and my ears stop burning, I realize: That's exactly why I like Cool Girl so much.

She says whatever is on her mind whenever it happens to be there.

With her, there are no soft or squishy words. No special treatment for the kid in the chair.

And absolutely, positively no editing.

NEW YUKS FOR NEW YORK

That night, tucked into my bedroom in the Smileys' garage, I'm straining my brain trying to come up with some new material.

The New York State finals at Gotham are coming at me like a speeding freight train. The kind without brakes. Or headlights.

And, get this: Gotham runs a summer camp for kids who want to be comics when they grow up. I've seen the brochure. They spend six weeks over the summer taking comedy classes from pros and doing campfire stand-up routines for one another. I'll be going up against kids who've spent most of their lives training for this one event—for them, it's the Funny People Olympics.

Thinking about the New York State round of the

competition has me scared. Not a little scared…
horror movie scared. Get-out-of-the-house-NOW-
because-he's-calling-you-from-downstairs-and-has-
a-chainsaw scared.

Maybe I should just quit while I'm ahead. I
won the first round. That should be enough.

But if I do that, everybody (except my loyal,
small, and somewhat geeky fan club) will always
say I won the Long Island competition because
the judges felt sorry for me.

So I need to press on. Show everybody that I'm
not a one-hit wonder.

I also need some new material. Most of the
people who'll be in the audience in New York
City have already seen my Ronkonkoma act on
YouTube. They know all the punch lines. They'll

probably remember the setups before I do, too.

So I'm mapping out a new routine. New jokes. Take some risks. Break new ground. Control my fear.

I have this idea about the local mall being an obstacle course or maybe a racetrack for me and my chair. It's like an indoor demolition derby.

Because for me to get from Cinnabon up in the food court down to Wicks 'n' Sticks on the first floor, I have to roll past two cell phone kiosks, avoid the kid throwing a tantrum outside Things R Us, maneuver around the horde of senior citizens doing a mall walk, find an elevator that isn't stuffed with shopping bags, avoid the perfume spritzers fogging the air outside every department store, sample some smoked sausage on toothpicks at Hickory Farms, get chased by Paul Blart, mall cop, on his Segway, and...

And this stinks.

It isn't funny!

So I scratch the whole thing and look up from my notebook. Because…

Stevie Kosgrov is in the driveway, leering at me through the garage door window.

"Good luck in round two, bro," he says with a smirk. "You poor, dumb loser!"

DYING IN THE LIVING ROOM

Okay. It's time for the torture test. A return engagement in the room where I bombed, big-time. Let's get ready to RUMBLE!

To get my confidence back, I'm going to do the unthinkable: I'm going to gather up all the Smileys in the living room and do exactly the same routine for them that was such a big hit with the audience and judges in Ronkonkoma.

If I can finally get through to them, if they laugh at just one of my jokes, then I'll be one hundred percent certain that winning the contest wasn't a fluke.

So on Friday night I give the Kosgrovs a special, one-night-only encore performance.

Except for Stevie. He's "out" with his friends.

I think he has a date to punch another goldfish.
Maybe a dolphin.

The Smileys are on the couch. I'm in front of
the TV, which, for the first time ever, is actually
switched off so they can watch me re-create my
Ronkonkoma magic!

I jump right in.

I do my quick intro—the Mrs. Darth Vader
substitute-teacher bit.

The Smileys stare at me. Blankly. Very, very
blankly.

I move on to the joke about how I got a ticket
for parking in the handicap parking space.

Uncle Smiley actually raises his hand.

"Yes, sir?" I say because I don't know what else
to do. No one has ever raised a hand during my
act before.

"How could you get a parking ticket?" he asks.
"You don't have a car."

"Or a driver's license, honey," adds Aunt Smiley.

"Don't you have to be sixteen to get one of
those?" asks their extremely logical youngest son.
"I think you do. I'm pretty sure you do, Jamie."

I could explain that their questions are what make the joke funny, but, well, if you have to explain 'em, they're not really jokes, are they?

So, sweating profusely and wondering why the Smileys decided to set the thermostat at ninety-nine point nine degrees tonight, I forge ahead to the zombie bit.

"The school crossing guard is a zombie?" screams the youngest Smiley. Then she starts crying. "I hugged her once, Mommy! Am I gonna turn into a zombie, too?"

"Take it easy, dear," says Aunt Smiley. "It's just a joke. I think. Right, Jamie?"

"Yeah," I say, blinking like crazy. There's a lot of sweat dribbling down my brow and into my eyes right now.

I do my Statue of Liberty bit. I pretend I'm holding up her torch and flash everybody my armpit, which is now so damp it resembles Lake Michigan.

I do some jokes about chicken nuggets, boogers, and appearing on *Dancing with the Stars*.

The Smileys just keep staring at me. Their eyes are glazing over. Their jaws are hanging open. They're not laughing or even smiling. The dog? He yawns, rolls over, and takes a nap. In the *middle* of a joke.

I skip the whole anti-PC bit, wave my hand over my head, and say, "Thank you. I'm Jamie Grimm. You've been a great crowd. Be sure to tip your waiters."

Uncle Smiley raises his hand again.

"Yes, sir?"

"We don't have any waiters."

I nod. "Yes, sir. I know."

And then, as a group, they give me their full critique:

We have to be honest with you, Jamie. We don't get it.

Chapter 50

THAT'S ALL, FOLKS!

So I quit.

Bet you didn't see that one coming, did you?

I don't want to be the punch line to somebody else's (Stevie Kosgrov's) joke. I just don't have what it takes to take this thing to the next level.

Saturday, at Frankie's diner, I stop telling jokes behind the cash register.

What? Not even a knock-knock joke?

"Here's your change, sir," I say glumly to my George Carlin–loving customer. "And?" he says with a big grin on his face, expecting his usual something extra.

"Have a nice day?"

"That's it? No Carlin? Not even a little Hippie-Dippie Weatherman?"

"Sorry. Not today. Probably not tomorrow, either. Probably not ever again."

My favorite Russian customer, Mr. Burdzecki, takes note of my attitude adjustment, too.

"No more Yakov Smirnoff?"

"Sorry. I'm all out."

He shakes his head sadly, like his best friend just died. "You not funny?"

"Yeah. I not funny."

"This is very sad day."

Tell me about it. It's not easy giving up on your dreams. But sometimes you just have to face facts. That thing you wanted to do more than anything in the world? People might be better off if you just didn't do it.

"Jamie?" says Uncle Frankie. "What's wrong?"

"Nothing much. I just don't want to tell jokes anymore."

"What? That's like me saying I don't want to yo-yo anymore."

"Well, maybe you should quit," I say. "It's not very safe. Or sanitary. You shouldn't fling that thing around the food all the time."

Yes, I'm being a big baby. I'm trying to make Uncle Frankie feel as bad as I do.

He shrugs. Keeps smiling. "Yo-yoing makes me happy."

"Well, it makes me nervous. The customers, too."

"Hey, kiddo, why don't you take a five-minute break?" he says, placing a gentle hand on my shoulder. "A friend of yours just came in."

He gestures toward a table with a big stack of books sitting on it.

Cool Girl is in the house.

Chapter 51

I'M OFFICIALLY OFF THE CLOCK

Why so glum, Grimm?" she asks.

I tell her what's going on. How I bombed again in the living room. How I know I'll bomb if I go on to the next round of the competition.

"Tell me a joke, Jamie," she says, folding her hands in her lap.

"You don't like it when I crack jokes."

"Yes, I do."

"What about that bit with the stopwatch?"

"I like you when you're not funny, too. But today I'm in the mood for some laughs. So, please, tell me a joke."

I rack my brain. Remember a quick Steven Wright one-liner. "Cross-country skiing is great—if you live in a small country."

Cool Girl laughs.

All right, it's a half laugh.

"I guess that wasn't a very good joke," I say.

"No, I liked it. Tell me another one."

And I do. George Carlin this time. "Ever notice that anyone going slower than you is an idiot, but anyone going faster is a maniac?"

Now she's really laughing.

I BRAKE FOR...
WAIT...AAAH!!
NO BRAKES!

So I tell her two or three more—mostly my own jokes. Now everybody in the diner, including Uncle Frankie and Mr. Burdzecki, wants to know what's so funny.

I push back from the table a little and start telling jokes to everybody in the diner.

They're laughing, and people out on the street want in on the action, too. So I roll out to the sidewalk and tell everybody in Long Beach a dozen or more jokes. Even the zombies are cracking up. They're laughing so hard, body parts are flying everywhere.

I've got my mojo back.

I funny.

I hope.

Because the New York State finals?

They're tomorrow. It's showtime!

Chapter 52

THE BIG (AND EXTREMELY CROWDED) DAY!

You know how heroes always rise up undaunted, never giving in to their fears or giving up on their courageous quests?

Well, I'm daunted. *Seriously daunted.*

In fact, I'm approaching "terrified" and well on my way to "scared silly."

I'm crammed inside the Smileys' SUV, stuck in the backseat, between Stevie and his younger brother. The smallest Smiley, their sister, is riding in the way-back with my folded-up chair.

We're going on a family outing to New York City to watch me die onstage in front of several hundred strangers.

Stevie couldn't be happier.

When we pull up in front of Gotham, I see Mrs. Kanai, my ELA teacher. Wow. She came into the city on a weekend to see me. How awesome is that?

As I'm swinging into my chair, I also see the vice principal. Mr. Sour Patch. He came, too? He

222

gives me another nod. This is major. I hope he gets a good seat. Maybe he can hang with the Smileys in the Frowning Section.

I enter the club and am completely blown away. Just about everybody I know is here to cheer me on. Uncle Frankie. The waitresses and busboys

from the diner. Mr. Burdzecki and his whole Russian family. Two cousins I didn't even know I had.

Yes, this time I've got my whole entourage.

And the nine other contestants hoping to win the title of New York State's Funniest Kid Comic?

They've brought everybody they've ever known, plus assorted unknown cousins, too.

There must be four, maybe five hundred people crammed inside the club. They're hanging from the rafters. It's the only way to see the stage from the back of the room.

I've never done my act in front of this many people. It's at least triple the size of the audience in Ronkonkoma.

With this many eyeballs staring at me, choke warnings are in full effect for the Tri-State area.

I nervous.

I extremely nervous.

Okay, I *petrified*.

MEETING THE PEOPLE
I'M GOING TO LOSE TO

And then I get even more petrified. Because backstage, in the holding room, I meet my competition.

As I listen to them talk, it sounds like all the other comics have been doing stand-up routines since they were in preschool. One sounds like he even did diaper jokes at his day care center.

Half of them have been to Komedy Kamp. Two have professional joke tutors. One of the girls, Judy from Manhattan, has what she calls a "development deal" with Disney to become the next Hannah Montana.

"Of course, it doesn't mean anything unless they, you know, actually 'develop' something," she adds.

I have no idea what she's talking about, but I know she's had way more experience than me.

We've just drawn numbers out of a hat to see what order we'll take the stage. I picked number ten. That means I'll be the last act up.

"Closing is good," says one of the other comics. "Unless you stink. Then it's stinky."

"I'd rather open," says this cocky comic from

Buffalo, who drew the first slot. "Why make 'em wait to hear the best material? You want to set the bar high, which I plan to do."

"Second from last is the primo position," says the guy who, coincidentally, will be going on second to last, right before me. His name is Shecky, and he comes from Schenectady, a town in upstate New York.

"Shecky's not my real name," he tells me later, when I'm sort of stuck in a corner between him and the couch. "I changed it because it sounds funny. 'Shecky from Schenectady.' Get it? Funny, no?"

"Yeah," I say.

"All words with *K* sounds in them are funny. Pickles. Cupcakes. Kazoos. Kumquats. All hilarious. You're Jamie Grimm, right?"

"Right. From Long Beach. Out on Long Island."

"You sure that's not Wrong Beach on Wrong Island?" He does an arm pump. "*Ba-boom*. See? I'm always riffing, always working on new material. Hey, seeing you in that wheelchair reminds me of a joke...."

"Um, maybe you should save it for when you're onstage," I suggest.

"Nah. That's okay. I got a million of 'em. Anyway, this doctor on Wrong Island gives a guy in a wheelchair six months to live. The wheelchair dude says he can't pay his bill, so the doctor gives him another six months. *Ba-boom!*"

I chuckle—not because Shecky's hilariously funny, but because, like I said, I'm sort of trapped. Besides, I already know most of his jokes. They're all straight out of the Henny Youngman joke book.

"This other doctor says to an old lady, 'Relax. You'll live to be eighty!' She says, 'I *am* eighty!' 'See?' says the doctor. 'I was right!'" Shecky does another arm chug. *"Ba-boom.* Nailed it."

"Erm, is that in your act?"

"Yep," he says, bouncing up on his heels and taking a deep breath because he's so sure he's going to win. "Those are but a few of the comedic morsels the audience will be savoring right before *you* go on. So don't be surprised if they're all laughed out when you roll onstage, Jamie baby."

"Thanks for the heads-up," I say.

"By the way…"

Shecky moves even closer so he can lean down and get in my face.

"If you were counting on getting sympathy votes from the judges, like you did out on Long Island, fuhgeddaboudit, *bubelah*."

"What? I didn't…"

Shecky from Schenectady holds up his hand to shush me.

Now I really wish my legs worked. So I could kick him.

"I read the blogs, babe. Trust me—that kind of pity play won't work in the Big Apple. These judges aren't softies, like the ones out on Wrong Island. So if you were thinking about racking up some more 'poor little cripple kid' points—sorry, babe. It's not gonna happen. Not today. You're goin' home with nothin' but a broken heart, which is perfect, because it'll match your broken body. *Ba-boom.* Nailed it!"

Oh yeah. I AM the funniest kid in the galaxy!

THE SHOW MUST GO ON
(SOMETIME SOON, PLEASE?)

It seems we're in the holding room for hours. I feel like a prisoner of war.

Or maybe that's just what spending two minutes with Shecky from Schenectady feels like. An eternity.

Then we're told that the start of the show is being delayed because the club needs to bring in more chairs for the overflow audience. Apparently, somebody's third cousins twice removed just arrived.

If this keeps up, our standing-room-only crowd is going to have to stand on top of each other.

"I'll bet they're waiting for Joe Amodio to show up," says Judy, the girl from Manhattan who might become a TV star on the Disney Channel.

"Who's Joe Amodio?" I ask.

"Executive producer of the Planet's Funniest Kid Comic Contest," she explains. "Whoever wins here goes on to the regionals up in Boston. If you win there, you move on to the semifinals in Vegas. You make it to the top four in Vegas, you're going to Hollywood."

"Hollywood?"

"The finals. Which, of course, will be televised. Live."

"Wow."

"Yeah. Nerve-racking, huh?"

"A little."

Actually, my sweat glands are kind of turning into lawn sprinklers again.

Shecky from Schenectady strolls over to butt in to our conversation.

"You guys talking about Hollywood?"

Before we even answer, he launches into another corny joke.

"Hey—what do you get when you cross a dog with a movie studio?"

Judy groans. "Collie-wood?"

"That's right, babe. And that's the kind of

killer material I'll be slaying the crowd with. Big-time. So maybe you two losers should just call it quits and head for home."

I grin. "What? And miss your act?"

Judy laughs. "Good one, Jamie."

I like Judy. If I don't win, I hope she does. And I hope she gets her Disney show, too.

"You know, Judy," says Shecky, puffing up his chest, "you're not a has-been. You're a never-was. I've seen your act, sister."

"Yeah, I know," says Judy. "And you stole half of it."

"I did not. Because your act is so lame, it makes this weenie in the wheelchair look like an Olympic sprinter. You started at the bottom, Judy, and it's been downhill ever since. *Ba-boom!* Nailed it."

The funny girl just shakes her head and waltzes away.

"You know," says Shecky, "that Judy is so dumb, she thinks a quarterback is a refund. She's so ugly..."

I don't stick around to hear the rest of his recycled "yo momma" jokes, because I see Aunt Smiley standing at the door.

"Hey," I say.

"Hi. I brought you a cold drink," she says, handing me an icy glass of water.

"Thanks." I gulp it down.

"It's crowded out there. Are you nervous?"

She's super worried. How can I tell? She's frowning even more than usual.

I nod. "Yeah. A little."

"Me too. And I'm not even the one going up onstage. Are you absolutely sure you want to go through with this, Jamie?"

I look over at Shecky from Schenectady.

"Yeah," I say. "More than ever."

"Okay," she says. "Just remember—the important thing is that you tried."

"Um, I haven't even lost yet."

"I know that. I'm talking about after."

Chapter 55

BATTER UP!

"Okay, that was Shecky from Schenectady," says the emcee. "Guess he forgot about our ten-minute time limit...."

Shecky totally tanked. He tried and tried, but all he got were a couple groans, like you hear when people repeat bad puns. I guess his friends and cousins couldn't make the trip down from Schenectady.

"Our next comic comes from Long Island," says the emcee. "He's from a town called Long Beach, which, if you ask me, is pretty obvious. Of course the beach is long—you just said it was on a *long* island. Makes you wonder, did the early settlers on Long Island forget to pack their adjectives? The only one they seem to know is *long*! 'This beach? Long beach. This guy? Longfellow. The boat ride over from England? *Long*.'"

The emcee is working hard. Trying to wake up the crowd that Shecky put to sleep. They chuckle. A little. Not a really great sign.

I'm waiting in the wings. Sweating up a storm. Getting ready to bolt.

"Okay, let's bring on our final comedian. Ladies and gentlemen, put your hands together for *Long* Island's very own Jamie Grimm."

The crowd roars. Well, *my* section roars. But today my section is pretty big.

I roll up a makeshift ramp to the stage.

I fiddle with the microphone stand, which both Shecky and the emcee forgot to lower, so it's about two feet too high.

And my brain freezes again. This time, I can't remember punch lines or setups. I'm even having trouble remembering my name and what day it is and exactly where I am and why.

Hands trembling, I fumble with the mic; twist it out of its clamp. While I'm doing all that, I look out at the audience and see my entourage. The Smileys. Uncle Frankie. The diner crew. Mrs. Kanai and my friends from school.

Cool Girl sees me seeing her and shoots me her coolest wink.

And suddenly my brain reboots.

"Um, hi," I say when I've finally wrestled the microphone free from the stand. "I'm Jamie Grimm. Maybe you saw my picture on the men's room door?"

I pivot sideways to give them a silhouette.

"By the way, have you ever really studied
a handicapped sign? If you tilt it sideways, it
sort of looks like a skinny guy with a ping-pong
ball head sliding down into a giant toilet bowl
because he forgot to lower the seat.

"Anyway, it's good to be here for the Planet's Funniest Kid Comic Contest. I hear there are elimination rounds going on today all over the known galaxy. Except on Vulcan. Those people don't laugh; they just live long and prosper."

The audience is laughing, so I improvise a quick bit on some other people who never laugh.

"I think my adoptive family is part Vulcan. They're here today. Very nice people, but they never, ever laugh. My apologies to all my fellow comics—those people who were *not* laughing at any of your jokes earlier? That would be my family."

The crowd laughs.

"And then there's my adoptive brother."

Yep. There's something about being alone in the spotlight that makes you feel like Superman a billion miles away from the nearest Kryptonite. I am actually going after Stevie Kosgrov!

"I wouldn't call him a bully. Let's just say he's mean as a snake. No offense to snakes. When he was a baby, he punched out a goldfish for looking at him the wrong way—which, you know, fish kind of have to do because their eyeballs are on the sides of their heads."

I do a funny fish face, and the audience cracks up.

"How mean is he? I'm thinking about getting a dog just so he'll have something to kick besides me. The other day I learned he's also a blogger, which, of course, is just two letters away from being a booger."

The audience applauds.

I smile.

Because now it's time to make fun of the people I actually like!

Standby for kamikaze comedy!

Chapter 56

BRINGING IT HOME!

"Then there's my Uncle Frankie," I say, gripping the mic with both hands. "What a guy. Champion yo-yoer. What? You've never heard of the Yo-Yo World Series? You watch. It'll be a sport at the next Olympics. My uncle runs a diner out in Long Beach."

There's a smattering of applause, led by Mr. Burdzecki and family.

"Oh, you've been there? Well, I should warn you—Uncle Frankie yo-yos while he cooks. His extra-crunchy biscuits? Baked yo-yos. His spaghetti? Used yo-yo strings. His Ring Dings? Chocolate-covered yo-yos."

I shield my eyes with one hand and peer into the crowd.

"Some of my friends from school are here today. Yep, there's my pal Pierce. The guy's a genius. He's so smart, he's counted to infinity. Twice. But, hey—the guy's a little nerdy. It's not like he's busy doing anything else."

The audience is really with me now. It feels better than guzzling a six-pack of Red Bull.

"And my other best friend is here, too. Gaynor. What can I tell you about Gaynor? The guy has a nose ring and tattoos. Couple of things you never want to hear in the tattoo parlor: 'Eagle? I thought you said *beagle*.' 'There are two *O*s in Bob, right?'"

"And then there's my new friend, a very cool girl from school. The other day she got super serious and asked me if I could take a whiz. I'm serious. She wanted to know if I could pee."

I toss up my hands to show how confused I was.

Then I imitate Cool Girl's voice. "'Be serious for five seconds, Jamie. I need to know. Can. You. Tinkle?' So I went ahead and made her day. I peed my pants."

Now the audience is howling.

I am so jazzed, I slam into a manic mash-up of all my best stuff—while popping wheelies on a few of the punch lines.

Illiterate? Write today for free help!
My friends say never listen, something like that.
If you can't laugh at yourself, I'll do it for you!

I do some funny accents, nailing Mr. Burdzecki on United Nations Beach.

I waddle out a few penguin jokes.

I make fun of the Smileys' dog.

I introduce the crowd to the zombies in the hood.

And since we're in New York City, I end with the Statue of Liberty.

The crowd goes crazy, erupting with laughter and applause.

Finally, it's time for me to take a bow.

And I do!

Because *I funny*!

LOOK AT ME! I'M THE COMEDY KING OF THE WORLD!

Cue the theme from *Rocky*!

It feels like the whole world is clapping and cheering for me. They won't let me leave the stage! The audience keeps screaming and making noise and chanting "Ja-mie, Ja-mie!"

The emcee finally rushes up and grabs the microphone.

"Ladies and gentlemen, Jamie Grimm! Jamie Grimm, ladies and gentlemen!"

The cheering gets louder. The chanting swells. "Ja-mie, Ja-mie, Ja-mie."

Now the three judges storm the stage. They're carrying a trophy!

"Ladies and gentlemen," says the head judge, "we're not gonna waste your time announcing runners-up and all that monkey junk. The decision of the judges was unanimous. The winner, the comic moving on to the regionals, the funniest kid comic in all of New York State is...the one, the only...Jamie Grimm!"

I take the trophy, hug it once, and wave to everybody.

It feels unbelievably great. It's a miracle. It's magical.

For a total of, maybe, fifteen seconds.

Chapter 58

CASUALTIES OF COMEDY

I can see my friends' and family's long faces from my spotlight on the stage.

The faces look even longer when I go into the audience and get the close-up view.

Prepare to die, funny boy!

IT'S LONELY AT THE TOP! (Especially if you stomp on your pals to get there)

Suddenly, I understand what I just did.

Remember how I said comedy was a great weapon to use against bullies? Well, it turns out it's a weapon so powerful that if you're not careful, it can also seriously injure the people you're closest to.

Gaynor and Pierce, my two best buds? The best guys ever. I've never seen them look sadder.

The Smileys are frowning even more than usual. Stevie, of course, is scowling at me.

Cool Girl? She's hiding it better than the others, but I can tell: She is totally crushed that I would take our private, extremely personal conversation and make fun of it. Who would do something like that? An insensitive idiot—that's who.

Poor Uncle Frankie. How could I say those mean things about him and his diner? He's the one who told me I had talent. Said I had a gift. And today I used it to trash his diner and his yo-yo—the two things he loves.

They all look so disappointed in me.

And, to be honest, I'm pretty disappointed in myself, too.

Was it worth hurting my true friends' feelings to win a dumb trophy? And what about Mrs. Kanai? I'd poked fun at her bleaching her facial hair. What'd she ever do to deserve that?

Today wasn't a school day, but I definitely learned a lesson: If I ever get up on a stage again (don't count on it), I will stay away from the mean-spirited stuff.

I will not make fun of my friends and family, who did nothing but support me.

I will never, ever be funny at the expense of people I care about.

Because if I don't care who my comedy hurts, I might as well change my name to Shecky and move to Schenectady.

Yeah, I funny.

But I also feel lousy.

Chapter 59

WAS IT SOMETHING I SAID?

The car ride back to Long Beach from Manhattan is very long and very, very quiet.

Once again, I'm crammed in the backseat between Stevie and his little brother.

Finally, when we're on the Long Island Expressway, Mary, the youngest Smiley, pops up in the way back and says, "Jamie? Remember that joke about bloggers and boogers?"

Stevie shoots me a look to let me know that I will soon be dead meat on a spit.

I gulp once and answer his little sister. "Yes?"

"That was *funny*."

"And we're Vulcans," says Uncle Smiley from behind the wheel.

In the passenger seat, Aunt Smiley holds up

her hand and spreads out her fingers like Spock.
"Live long and prosper."

Then the two of them, believe it or not, start
laughing.

It's a miracle.

They do laugh! It just takes them about an hour to get the joke. It's like they have a built-in time delay on their funny bones.

"And that bit about Frank with his yo-yos!" Aunt Smiley giggles. "That was priceless."

"I always wondered why his biscuits tasted like hockey pucks," adds Uncle Smiley.

"Ooh," says Aunt Smiley. "Hoo. Ooh-hoo."

I think she's building up to an actual "ha-ha-ha."

"I liked when you made the funny fish face!" says Stevie's little brother. "Mom, Dad," he says in a deep dumb voice, which must be how he thinks his big brother sounds. "I'm going to the pet store to punch a goldfish *and* a guppy!"

Up front, Aunt and Uncle Smiley giggle. The two little Smileys chuckle.

Finally, I pipe up. "So, um, you guys aren't mad at me?"

"Of course not!" says Aunt Smiley. "Tee-hee. We haven't laughed this hard in ages. Hee."

Even though she sounds like an embarrassed bird when she titters, she's making me feel way better. I guess all is forgiven.

"You sure?" I say. "You're not just saying I was funny because you don't want to hurt my feelings?"

"Of course not, Jamie," says Aunt Smiley. "You *were* funny."

"Funny-looking, too," says Stevie's little brother.

"You keep making that fish face," adds his mother, "and it *will* stick."

"I think it already has!" cracks Uncle Smiley.

They all do their bird laughs again. *Tee-hee, tee-hee.*

"Oh," says Aunt Smiley, "I heard a good wheelchair joke the other day."

Okay. This is more like it. They're making fun of me. That's fair. Lay it on me.

"Let's see," says Aunt Smiley, trying to remember her joke.

I can relate to that.

"Oh. Right. Two vultures were sitting in a tree. One sees a man in a wheelchair rolling down a hill. He taps the other vulture and says, 'Why, look, Fred. Meals on Wheels!'"

Okay. It's awful. But the other Smileys (except Stevie, of course) are still *tee-hee-hee*ing.

When we pull into Smileyville, everybody is there. Gaynor, Pierce, Gilda, and Cool Girl. Mrs. Kanai and the vice principal. Uncle Frankie and the gang from the diner.

"Surprise!" they all shout.

"It's a party!" cries Uncle Frankie, hoisting up

a huge bottle of orange soda. "To celebrate the funniest kid in all of New York State. My nephew, the one and only Jamie Grimm! But instead of ice cream and cake, we're having chocolate-covered yo-yos!"

Yes, he swung by the grocery store and bought every box of Ring Dings and Ding Dongs he could find.

Guess he's forgiven me, too.

"You know the secret to staying young, Jamie?" says Uncle Frankie.

"Yo-yoing while you cook? Your fish-oil capsules?"

He shakes his head. "Nope. Being able to laugh at yourself. So thanks for keeping me young, kiddo."

What a party. What a night.

The best I've had in two years.

The best since the night I lost everything and everybody I ever loved.

Chapter 60

AN EVEN BIGGER (AND BETTER) SURPRISE

The next day things go back to normal.

Zombies in the neighborhood, school, a couple of jokes in math class, mystery meat in the cafeteria.

In other words, life is mostly pretty good. As life goes.

That night, Cool Girl and I meet up on the boardwalk. Just to sit and chat. So we chit. Then we chat. I bet we could chitchat (and chatchit) all night long and still have stuff to talk about when the sun came up, because when I'm with Cool Girl, I feel free to talk about anything and everything.

And she'll listen.

And then she'll tell me all sorts of incredibly weird stuff and ask the most insanely bizarre

questions. Like I said before, with her there is no editing.

So I'm trying to be more like that. Just blurt out whatever's on my mind.

Like *the operation.*

"The doctors say there's an operation I could have."

"And you could walk again?"

"Yeah."

"Cool!"

"I guess," I say. "But it's supposed to be dangerous. It could, you know, make things even worse. Paralyze more junk." I move my hand up from my lap to my waist to my chest.

She gets the picture. "Oh. Not cool."

"Yeah. Plus no insurance company would ever pay for it, anyway. It's what they call an 'experimental procedure.'"

"Would it paralyze your lips?"

"Huh?"

"This operation. Would it make your lips go all limp and floppy?"

I shrug. "I don't know. No? I guess if they cut the wrong nerve or something..."

"Well," she says, scooting to the edge of the bench, moving in so close I could count the freckles on her face if I wasn't so busy staring into her eyes. "I don't want to risk it."

I swallow hard. "Risk what?"

"Missing this."

She closes her eyes and kisses me.

It's soft. Gentle. Unbelievably gentle, actually. And it's over way too quickly.

But I'll never forget it. Never, ever, ever. Even if I have that operation and it paralyzes my brain.

Because you never forget your first real kiss. Well, not me, anyway.

Hey, I'm just a kid from Cornball, remember?

Chapter 61

REMEMBERING ANOTHER NIGHT

"**I** guess I'd better head home," says Cool Girl after we both sigh and gaze at the twinkling stars for a while.

"I'll walk you," I say.

She laughs. "I thought you said that would require a medical miracle."

"True," I say as we shove off. "And, like I said, insurance companies aren't big on paying for miracles."

We make our way up the boardwalk. She rests her hand on my shoulder. This is how we can stroll hand in hand while my actual hands are busy pumping rubber.

She really is a good friend. I trust her in a way I don't trust anybody else.

And so I finally tell her.

"It was at night," I say.

"What was?"

"What happened. The car wreck. We were driving along the Storm King Highway."

"Where's that?"

"Oh, it's one of the most scenic drives in the whole state," I say, somewhat sarcastically. "Route 218. The road that connects West Point and Cornwall up in the Highlands on the west side of the Hudson River. It's narrow and curvy and hangs off the cliffs on the side of Storm King Mountain. An extremely twisty two-lane road. With a lookout point and a picturesque stone wall to stop you from tumbling off into the river. Motorcycle guys love Route 218."

We stop moving forward and pause under a streetlamp.

"But if you ask me, they shouldn't let trucks use that road."

Cool Girl looks at me. "Go on, Jamie," she says gently.

And so I do.

"Like I said, it was night. And it was raining. We'd gone to West Point to take the tour, have a picnic. It was a beautiful day. Not a cloud in the sky until the tour was over, and then it started pouring. Guess we stayed too late. Me, my mom, my dad." Now I bite back the tears. "My little sister. Jenny. You would've liked Jenny. She was always happy. Always laughing.

"We were on a curve. All of a sudden, this truck comes around the side of the cliff. It's halfway in our lane and fishtailing on account of the slick road. My dad slams on the brakes. Swerves right. We smash into a stone fence and bounce off it like we're playing wall ball. The hood of our car slides under the truck, right in front of its rear tires— tires that are smoking and screaming and trying to stop spinning."

I see it all again. In slow motion.

The detail never goes away.

"They all died," I finally say. "My mother, my father, my little sister. I was the lucky one. I was the only one who survived."

I AM THE LUCKY ONE

Now that I've finally started talking about it, I can't stop.

"Believe it or not, the truck driver wasn't hurt at all—even though his cab slammed into the cliff and the nose of his big rig crumpled like something in a cartoon. He was the one who called 9-1-1.

"While we waited for the police to show up, he kept circling close to me, kept telling me he was *so* sorry and how he hadn't seen us coming.

"The state police came. And then an ambulance. Fire trucks. I remember the flares and lots of swirling, flashing lights. The paramedics told me not to move. To keep my head perfectly still. That's when I realized I *couldn't* move. At least, not my legs.

"While they were working on me, steadying

my head, moving me to the backboard, I kept asking people, 'Where's my sister? You have to find my sister.'"

Cool Girl is kneeling beside me now. She wraps her arms around me and holds me tight. "I'm here," she says. "I'm right here."

"They told me to calm down. Not to move. I was flat on my back, and the raindrops kept falling straight down at me. 'Where's Jenny?' I kept asking. Finally, a police officer in a Smokey Bear hat all wrapped in wet plastic leaned in and told me, 'She didn't make it, son.' That's when I blacked out, I think. I don't remember anything else. Except for the rain. It kept falling into my eyes, washing away my tears."

Cool Girl squeezes me harder. She holds me like she'll never let me go. She holds me like I've needed to be held since that horrible night out on the side of Storm King Mountain.

She's crying for me, I guess.

I'm crying for my mom and dad, and for my little sister, Jenny.

BACK TO SEMI-NORMAL

After I pour my heart out to Cool Girl, I actually feel better.

You think I should've done it sooner? Maybe you're right. I guess I just wasn't ready to talk about what happened. It was hard to talk. I'm glad it's over.

The next morning my life begins a slow but steady return to its pleasant subnormal (and somewhat abnormal) normality.

At school my buddies are the best.

Gilda has put together a list of comedy concert DVDs for us to watch.

"All the best stand-ups," she says. "You can study their moves and timing before you go on to the regionals. These can be your training films."

Pierce and Gaynor and I still hang out whenever

we can. But now every time Gaynor does something remotely goofy, he says, "Are you gonna put that in your act? You should, man. Because it's so stupid, it'd be funny. Are you gonna put it in your act?"

Turns out he actually enjoys being the butt of some of my jokes.

"It makes me famous," he says, "and girls dig famous people. Trust me on that."

At home the Smileys are acting kind of human around me. Except Stevie. I think it's technically impossible for him to act human (because he isn't one).

They *almost*, kind of, occasionally, more or less get my jokes. It just takes about an hour. Sometimes longer.

"Oh," says Uncle Smiley, "I get it now. The Ring Dings Frank serves at his diner are chocolate-covered yo-yos because both objects are round and about the same size and width, and he likes to play with yo-yos. Oh-ho. That's funny. Very amusing."

Aunt Smiley is a much better actor. She also took the time to look up a lot of different ways to tell me I'm funny.

"You're hysterical, Jamie!" Or "That's a real knee-slapper, Jamie!" And "My, Jamie, what a waggish, witty, and whimsical way with words!"

Yep. I not only funny.

I jolly, comical, and humorous, too.

So things are definitely looking up in Smileyville.

Even Ol' Smiler is grinning most of the time.

I am definitely the luckiest guy I know.

Chapter 64

ZOMBIES ON PARADE!

So did being crowned New York State's Funniest Kid Comic change my life?

A little. Couldn't hurt, right? Better than a sharp stick in the eye.

For instance, one morning the zombies all got together and carried me to school.

They said my act was so funny (they caught it on SpookTube), they laughed their butts off.

And talk about applause. When these guys give you a hand, *they give you a hand*.

Fortunately, none of the zombies wanted to eat me.

"You a comedian," one drooling ghoul grumbled. "You taste funny."

Chapter 65

MOB SCENE BY THE SEA

That Saturday, when I head over to Uncle Frankie's Good Eats by the Sea, there is a line out the door because so many people want to come in and congratulate me behind the cash register.

Maybe you've seen the satellite photos.

The line is about ten miles long, and every person in it wants one joke from me and one chocolate-covered yo-yo from Uncle Frankie.

There are so many people on the streets of Long Beach that the president of the United States calls because he's worried we might exceed the island's weight limit and all end up at the bottom of the ocean with SpongeBob.

Not really, guys.

There is no such thing as SpongeBob.

Or a line that long.

But Mr. Burdzecki is sitting on a stool at the counter all day so he can share a few words with any new customers who meet me for the first time: "Jamie Grimm? He funny!"

I knew him when he was nobody except my friend.

Chapter 66

A SUNDAY DRIVE INTO MY PAST

On Sunday the Smileys take me and Cool Girl upstate to visit the place I called home right before I moved to Smileyville.

The Hope Trust Children's Rehabilitation Center.

What we patients all called the Hopeless Hotel.

It's a special hospital for kids who've been in horrible accidents or have other kinds of super-serious medical conditions. It's where I spent nearly a year recovering from the "severe trauma" of the car wreck. Hope Trust is totally supported by private money. I don't think anyone hosts a telethon for it, but someone should. Maybe someday I will.

As we cruise the corridors, I see some of my old friends.

Like Carly. She has myotubular myopathy. It makes her muscles weak. A lot of kids who have it die before they're one. Carly is eight. She's what you might call a "fighter."

Easy, Carly! I don't want to break my ribs. Again.

She's been checking in and out of Hope Trust her whole life. This is where she learned how to walk.

"You'll get there, too, Jamie," she says.

"Thanks."

"Jamie?"

I can't believe it. When I was at Hope Trust, Derek, who's seventeen, couldn't walk or talk. Heck, he could barely breathe. I remember he had so many tubes coming out of his body, some of the other kids called him Scuba Dude. Derek had been tossed out of a car, just like me. But while I landed on my butt, Derek landed on his head. As a result, he more or less sprained his brain and ended up with all sorts of neurological damage.

Now he's walking with a cane and talking.

"Good to see you, man," says Derek.

"You too."

"Remember when I was, like, totally zonked out, and all you kids called me Scuba Dude?"

"Um, yeah?"

"I heard that, man. I heard every word." He winks and smiles. We knock knuckles. "I'm late for PT."

"En-*joy*."

"Yeah, like that's gonna happen...."

I remember PT. Physical therapy. It's like gym class, but with a little medieval torture action tossed in.

Hey, I can't complain. PT is what got me out of that bed and into this chair.

Okay. I guess we shouldn't have called this place the Hopeless Hotel. But we all did. Mostly because we all thought we were hopeless cases until someone, usually a doctor or a nurse or a physical therapist, showed us we weren't.

"I want you to see something," I say to Cool Girl.

I take her to the hospital's patient library. One whole section of the bookshelves is crammed with joke books.

"The doctors and nurses up here always said, 'Laughter is the best medicine.' So they'd bring me a couple of these books, and every day I'd read all I could about comedians and jokes and comedy sketches. Even when nobody thought I'd live, I kept reading joke books. And you know what?"

"What?"

"I think all that laughing is what kept me alive."

Chapter 67

LAUGHTER REALLY IS THE BEST MEDICINE

We meet up with the Smileys again in the hospital cafeteria. You know, the Smileys are turning out to be good people. With one major exception, of course.

The place is packed. It's wall-to-wall wheelchairs and walkers and medical people dressed in pastel-colored scrubs. I scan the tables, and all I see are tired medical workers, scared parents, and sad kids.

I see myself a year ago.

The place is totally quiet except for a few coughs and the clink of silverware on plates.

"Not exactly like Gotham," whispers Cool Girl out of the side of her mouth.

288

I sigh—then I start to grin. "Says who? Give me a hand, you guys. Need just a little help."

Cool Girl, the Smileys, this orderly I remember named Bob, and, yes, *even Stevie* all grab hold of my chair, hoist me up, and prop me on top of an empty table.

"Good afternoon, ladies and gentlemen. My name is Jamie Grimm. I don't know if you heard about it, but maybe a week ago, some idiots in New York City named me the funniest stand-up comedian kid in all of New York. I have one question for those judges: Are you people blind? I haven't stood in over a year."

A few chuckles ripple through the cafeteria.

"I live in Long Beach. That's on Long Island. We're famous for our zombies. The other day, I was rolling to school, and this one zombie says to his friend, 'Mmmmm. Loooook. Meals on wheels.'"

Now they're laughing. I shoot Aunt Smiley a wink to thank her for the assist on my new material.

I do a quick riff on Pierce and Gaynor, crack a couple of booger jokes, and do a whole bit on Uncle Frankie getting his own *Cooking With Yo-Yos* show on the Food Network. I even have some fun

When I was here, my doctors gave me pills for my B.O. Unfortunately, they kept slipping out from under my arms!

with Stevie Kosgrov. Now I have him working his way up, Rocky-style, from boxing with goldfish to taking on a tuna. "And to become heavyweight champion of the undersea world, he's getting ready to whale on a whale."

There's a ton more laughter. The best I've ever heard.

And then I launch into a skit I've been working on in secret for a couple of weeks.

"I came here in the summer. Some kids go to camp—paddle canoes and get a whistle lanyard. Not me. I came *here*, did PT, and got my own personal bedpan. I remember that thing was *sooooo* cold. Once, I asked my nurse if she stored my bedpan in the refrigerator. She said, 'Yes. If we put it in the freezer, it tears off too much skin.'"

A nurse in the cafeteria—one of the women who took such good care of me—is laughing so hard, she's holding her sides.

"So," I say, "do you guys still call this place the Hopeless Hotel?"

"Yeah!" a bunch of kids shout out. Others are nodding their heads. Some are clapping.

"Well, it *is* a lot like a hotel. It's got tons of rooms and a heated swimming pool. Plus, a very friendly staff. There are all sorts of people standing by in the lobby to carry stuff up to your rooms. They'll even carry *you*. This guy over here? Bob? He lifted me in and out of my bed so many times I felt like I was his personal set of dumbbells. I know he loved it when I was in that heavy plaster cast. Gave him a good workout. Really pumped up his biceps. I should've charged him a gym fee."

Bob is laughing and clapping and showing everybody his bulging arm muscles.

"So, okay, the Hopeless Hotel is definitely a hotel. But that 'hopeless' part? I'm not so sure about that anymore.

"See, earlier, out in the halls, I ran into my friends Carly and Derek." I slap the sides of my wheelchair. "I really need to find the brakes on this thing. Anyway, I ran into them, and guess what? They're both doing way better—even after a lot of people gave up on them. But not their families. Not their friends. And, most important, not themselves.

"You ever hear this old expression: When the world says 'Give up,' hope whispers 'Try it one more time'? Neither had I. Not until I came here, and some anonymous night nurse scribbled it on my cast. With a Sharpie. We're talking permanent ink, people. That little slogan didn't come off until the cast did. But the hope? I still got it. Big-time. In fact, right now I'm hoping some of you guys will help me get down off this table. Otherwise, I'm stuck up here, and I left my freezing-cold bedpan at home."

I wave my hand over my head.

"Thank you! I'm Jamie Grimm. And you've been the best audience in the world!"

They clap and cheer, and I know in my heart it doesn't get any better than this.

This one moment, here at the Hopeless Hotel, beats everything else in my whole story. Winning the contests in Ronkonkoma and Manhattan. Saturdays at Uncle Frankie's. Goofing around with Gaynor and Pierce.

Yes, it even tops my first kiss.

I can't explain exactly why. It just does!

Chapter 68

AND NOW A WORD FROM OUR TORMENTOR

When I'm down off the cafeteria table, Stevie Kosgrov comes up to me.

Guess he didn't like that whole "whale on a whale" routine. Do I blame him? Nah. Maybe. Well, yeah.

I scrunch up my face and tighten my stomach muscles so I'm ready to take a good punch.

But Stevie totally surprises me.

Instead of slugging me, he puts out his hand. A little nervous, I take it.

"We're not friends, though," he says as we shake.

"Definitely not," I say. "We're mortal enemies."

"To the death, bro. Sooner or later, you're going down."

"Maybe. But you know what, Stevie?"

"What?"

"Sooner or later, I'll get right back up again, too."

Chapter 69

THE ROAD TO WHATEVER COMES NEXT!

So, what happens next?

Well, I'm not exactly sure, because it hasn't happened yet. But here's a little trailer for things you can *maybe* (kind of, sort of) expect in the next book:

It's on to Boston and the Northeast Regionals for yours truly, where—who knows?— maybe I'll be up against Billy Crystal's extremely funny nephew *and* a hilarious, wisecracking dog. Hey, who could beat a dog? I'm already sweating just making it up.

Maybe in the next book, Uncle Frankie will teach me how to do Around the World with a yo-yo in one hand while simultaneously plopping pickles on hamburger buns with the other.

What else? Let's see....

Cool Girl gives me another kiss.

Gilda Gold gives me a kiss.

And Stevie Kosgrov socks me in the kisser.

I get a congratulatory call from the president. Of Russia. "You funny, *da*?" he says.

"*Da*," I say. "I funny."

Lots of stuff like that in the next book. Plus, a lot more jokes.

If there is a next book.

I mean, what if I lose? What if I bomb in Boston? What if I make it to the semifinals in Las Vegas but not all the way to Hollywood?

I definitely need to think about something to fall back on besides my butt, because I don't want to break any more butt bones.

Hey, maybe I could write movies for Adam Sandler.

Or if laughter really is the best medicine, maybe I could become a doctor and hang out at the Hopeless Hotel.

I know one thing for sure: I won't give up. Hope will keep whispering in my ear, telling me to get up and try one more time.

And I will.

Even though I totally agree with what Steven Wright says: "You can't have everything. Where would you put it?"

Hey, thanks for hanging out and reading my story. Until next time, I'm Jamie Grimm. I'm the luckiest kid in the world.

And for now, at least, I'm the funniest kid in New York!

P.S. FROM JAMIE

Have you ever wanted to crack up your friends and family? Well, the first thing you're going to need are some can't-miss jokes. The Web is full of sites that'll help you get started. Here are some of my favorites:

kids.yahoo.com/jokes
bconnex.net/~kidworld/weekjoke.htm
ahajokes.com/kids_jokes.html
jokesbykids.com
kids.niehs.nih.gov/games/jokes/jokes_galore.htm
ducksters.com/jokesforkids

Jamie's comic quest continues in...

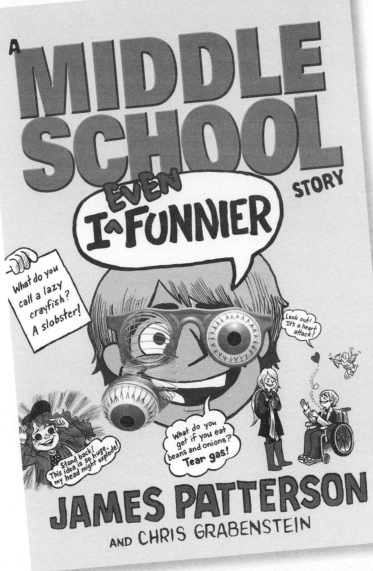

Read on for an extract

Chapter 1

IT'S FUN BEING FUNNY

Hi! I'm Jamie Grimm, and it's really great to be back in front of an audience again.

A little while back, I won a couple of contests and was crowned the Funniest Kid Comic in all of New York. Not just New York City, but the whole state!

Now I have a shot at being the Planet's Funniest Kid Comic.

"The planet Earth?" asks Phineas of—you guessed it—*Phineas and Ferb*. "Or Mars? We built a portal to Mars for the science fair once."

"Fun never falls too far from the tree house," adds Ferb.

Yep! Phineas and Ferb, the two hysterical stars from the Disney Channel, are now my close personal friends. They even go to school with me.

Derek Jeter, the shortstop from the New York Yankees, shows up at Long Beach Middle School because he wants *me* to autograph a baseball for *him*.

Taylor Swift comes to town to ask me to be the opening act at her upcoming concerts. "Jamie Grimm, I hear you're the Planet's Funniest Kid Comic!"

"Not exactly," I tell her. "First I have to win a regional competition in Boston. And then there are the semifinals in Las Vegas. And the final finals in Hollywood…"

"He's going to be a very busy boy," says Howie Mandel, one of the judges from *America's Got Talent*. He's come to Long Beach to help me train for the comedy competition. "Jamie needs new material. New jokes. A new hairdo. You like mine?"

Of course my best buds—Jimmy Pierce, Joey Gaynor, and Gilda Gold—are with me, too. We're on our way to school, where the principal has declared that today is Jamie Grimm Day.

"They're gonna give you your very own pep rally, dude," says Gaynor.

So after the cheerleaders do a "Jay-mee Grimm"

cheer, our school principal, Dr. Heinz Doofenshmirtz, or Doof as he likes to call himself, starts to make a little speech.

"Wait a second," says Phineas. "Your principal is *our* evil scientist?"

I shrug. "I guess he likes the cafeteria food."

Dr. Doofenshmirtz goes on with the quick speech. "Today, Jamie, we gather here to wish you luck as you prepare to take the second, third, and fourth steps toward your goal of being the Planet's Funniest Kid Comic! Break a leg, Jamie. Whoopsie!"

When Principal Doof says that, I know this has to be a dream.

Because, you know, all those steps he mentioned? I'd be happy just taking one.

Chapter 2

MEANWHILE, BACK IN REALITY...

Sometimes people in my dreams say crazy dumb stuff because they forget I'm in a wheelchair.

Hey, I don't blame 'em. I'd like to forget it, too. But I can't.

Of course, I keep hoping that one day I'll see a commercial for a new wonder drug called something like Spinulax that will magically make me walk again. Unfortunately, it would probably come with a list of gross side effects like all those other pills they advertise on TV: *"Spinulax may cause constipation and diarrhea. Not to mention projectile vomiting. And sudden death syndrome—as in, oops, sorry, you're dead."*

When I wake up, I'm in my bedroom. In the

garage. Back in the real world. And I need to get my butt ready for school.

About my bedroom in the garage…when I moved to Long Beach to live with my aunt and uncle, the only spare room in the house wasn't actually *in* the house. This is why my clothes often smell like a Home Depot.

I call my aunt and uncle's house Smileyville because when I first got here, nobody ever smiled. Not even the dog, Ol' Smiler. He hadn't wagged his tail in so long his butt was brittle.

Anyway, I think I've finally figured out why the Smileys always look so glum.

It's the oat gruel.

That's what Mrs. Smiley serves for breakfast, *every morning*. You know how they say breakfast will stick with you? Well, her oat gruel sure will. It'll stick to your teeth and the roof of your mouth. *All day long.*

Quick, somebody call one of those cable TV networks! I have an awesome idea for a new reality show: *Breakfast With the Smileys!* It'll be the exact opposite of those shows about the Kardashians or the Real Housecats of Beverly Hills. No glitz. No glamour. No nothing.

"Have a nice day," says my aunt, Mrs. Smiley.

"Don't forget your lunch," my uncle, Mr. Smiley, reminds me.

"Be home by six," Aunt Smiley adds.

Yep. They're even blander than oat gruel.

But they took me into their home when I had no place else to go.

And for that, I will always be grateful.

No joke.

Chapter 3

GUESS WHAT I SAW THIS MORNING?

As I'm heading up the sidewalk on my way to school, I see this really big, really green garbage truck grinding its way through something much worse than my aunt's oat gruel. We're talking mushy, juicy slop, slimier than the food scraps and sour milk sloshing around in the plate-scraper's barrel at my middle school's cafeteria.

And I start thinking about adding this to my comedy act....

If Long Beach wants a big green monster to gobble up its garbage, they should hire Godzilla. I hear they kicked the big guy out of Japan.

Something to do with him yanking the tops off too many Tokyo skyscrapers and munching on them like they were Nestlé Crunch bars. I think Godzilla ate a few subway sandwiches, too. The kind made out of *real* subway cars.

If Godzilla moved to Long Beach, he could stomp on down the streets, scooping up and emptying out Dumpsters. Even with his monstrous screeches, he'd be quieter than the guys who usually show up on our street at six AM to do drum solos on everybody's trash cans. Thanks to the garbagemen, nobody on our block needs an alarm clock.

Of course, if Godzilla did move to Long Beach, every time he went to, say, an all-you-can-eat buffet, a dozen waiters would probably disappear.

And you know what you'd find between Godzilla's toes?

Slow runners. (Sorry, I couldn't resist that one.)

When I meet up with Gilda Gold at the end of the block, I tell her my Godzilla the Garbageman idea.

She laughs and whips out her iPhone.

"That would make an awesome short," she says, starting to record. "We just shoot the garbage truck chewing up trash but dub in monster-movie music and really loud sound effects."

"And voices," I say. "Make 'em sound like they're coming from people buried underneath the garbage. *'Help meeeee!'*"

Gilda laughs.

I smile.

Gilda has a really cool laugh. A whole room can be cracking up, but you'll always hear her amazing giggle rippling through it all. It's the kind of laugh that makes a kid want to keep on telling jokes for the rest of his life just so he can keep hearing it.

Yep. Gilda's laugh is one of the reasons I want to be a stand-up comic more than anything in the world—even if I don't exactly fit the job description.

HIGH ADVENTURE ON THE HIGH SEAS!

Turn the page for a sneak peek at
James Patterson's new series.

1

L et me tell you about the last time I saw my
dad.

We were up on deck, rigging our ship to ride
out what looked like a perfect storm.

Well, it was perfect if you were the storm.
Not so much if you were the people being tossed
around the deck like wet gym socks in a washing
machine.

We had just finished taking down and tying
off the sails so we could run on bare poles.

"Lash off the wheel!" my dad barked to my big
brother, Tailspin Tommy. "Steer her leeward and
lock it down!"

"On it!"

Tommy yanked the wheel hard and pointed our bow downwind. He looped a bungee cord through the wheel's wooden spokes to keep us headed in that direction.

"Now get below, boys. Batten down the hatches. Help your sisters man the pumps."

Tommy grabbed hold of whatever he could to steady himself and made his way down into the deckhouse cabin.

Just then, a monster wave lurched over the starboard side of the ship and swept me off my feet. I slid across the slick deck like a hockey puck on ice. I might've gone overboard if my dad hadn't reached down and grabbed me a half second before I became shark bait.

"Time to head downstairs, Bick!" my dad shouted in the raging storm as rain slashed across his face.

"No!" I shouted back. "I want to stay up here and help you."

"You can help me more by staying alive and not

letting *The Lost* go under. Now hurry! Get below."

"B-b-but—"

"Go!"

He gave me a gentle shove to propel me up the tilting deck. When I reached the deckhouse, I grabbed onto a handhold and swung myself around and through the door. Tommy had already headed down to the engine room to help with the bilge pumps.

Suddenly, a giant sledgehammer of salt water slammed into our starboard side and sent the ship tipping wildly to the left. I heard wood creaking. We tilted over so far I fell against the wall while our port side slapped the churning sea.

We were going to capsize. I could tell.

But *The Lost* righted itself instead, the ship tossing and bucking like a very angry beached whale.

I found the floor and shoved the deckhouse hatch shut. I had to press my body up against it. Waves kept pounding against the door. The water definitely wanted me to let it in.

That wasn't going to happen. Not on my watch.

I cranked the door's latch to bolt it tight.

I would, of course, reopen the door the instant my dad finished doing whatever else needed to be done up on deck and made his way aft to the cabin. But, for now, I had to stop *The Lost* from taking on any more water.

If that was even possible.

The sea kept churning. *The Lost* kept lurching. The storm kept sloshing seawater through every crack and crevice it could find.

Me? I started panicking. Because I had a sinking feeling (as in "We're gonna sink!") that this could be the end.

I was about to be drowned at sea.

Is twelve years old too young to die?

Apparently, the Caribbean Sea didn't think so.